EXTINCT

THE GREAT DYING BOOK ONE

JACK HUNT

DIRECT RESPONSE PUBLISHING

ISBN: 9798483406761

For my Family

ALSO BY JACK HUNT

If you haven't joined ***Jack Hunt's Private Facebook Group*** just do a search on facebook to find it. This gives readers a way to chat with Jack, see cover reveals, enter contests and receive giveaways, and stay updated on upcoming releases. There is also his main facebook page below if you want to browse. facebook.com/jackhuntauthor

Go to the link below to receive special offers, bonus content, and news about new Jack Hunt's books. Sign up for the newsletter. http://www.jackhuntbooks.com/signup

The Great Dying series

Extinct

Primal

Species (coming November)

A Powerless World series

Escape the Breakdown

Survive the Lawless

Defend the Homestead

Outlive the Darkness

Evade the Ruthless

Outlaws of the Midwest series

Chaos Erupts

Panic Ensues

Havoc Endures

The Cyber Apocalypse series

As Our World Ends

As Our World Falls

As Our World Burns

The Agora Virus series

Phobia

Anxiety

Strain

The War Buds series

War Buds 1

War Buds 2

War Buds 3

Camp Zero series

State of Panic

State of Shock

State of Decay

Renegades series

The Renegades

The Renegades Book 2: Aftermath

The Renegades Book 3: Fortress

The Renegades Book 4: Colony

The Renegades Book 5: United

The Wild Ones Duology

The Wild Ones Book 1

The Wild Ones Book 2

The EMP Survival series

Days of Panic

Days of Chaos

Days of Danger

Days of Terror

Against All Odds Duology

As We Fall

As We Break

The Amygdala Syndrome Duology

Unstable

Unhinged

Survival Rules series

Rules of Survival

Rules of Conflict

Rules of Darkness

Rules of Engagement

Lone Survivor series

All That Remains

All That Survives

All That Escapes

All That Rises

Single Novels

Blackout

Defiant

Darkest Hour

Final Impact

The Year Without Summer

The Last Storm

The Last Magician

The Lookout

Class of 1989

Out of the Wild

The Aging

Mavericks: Hunters Moon

Killing Time

1

Thursday, April 28
Albany, New York

The single hundred-dollar bill was hard to ignore.

Over two hundred students in the tiered seating of a lecture hall in the State University of New York at Albany stared in bemusement at it. It had been attached to a chalkboard for the duration of her class without any mention of its purpose until now.

Above it, scribbled in white chalk, a quote.

Professor Emily Mansfield leaned back against her desk, waiting for an answer. She was thirty-eight, three years younger than her new boyfriend. She had a clean, timeless look about her: high cheekbones and flashing green eyes with sharp features that matched her athletic appearance. That morning she was wearing a white shirt beneath a light brown cardigan, dark slacks, and sensible flat shoes. A black briefcase was open full of marked papers. Nearby was a silver thermos set on the desk.

"Would anyone else like to take another guess?" A pause. No response.

She swept a few strands of long auburn hair out of her face then pushed away from the desk and pointed to the money. "A hundred dollars. No one? Come on, guys. You've been in and out of this room most of the semester. Surely someone noticed. If anyone can tell me what is different about this room, the money is yours. It's that simple."

There were only two people other than her who knew, and one had sworn to say nothing and the other was still oblivious. Emily winked at her twelve-year-old daughter Anna, sitting near the front. She was the youngest in the room. Her hazel eyes twinkled in her face framed by shoulder-length dark curls and dotted with a few freckles. It was Take Your Child to Work Day.

Amar, a student in the back of the room, had pointed it out a few times over the past few weeks but at that moment not even he was connecting the dots. Emily strolled in front of her students; hands clasped in front of her. When she could see they were stumped, she made her way to the exit and flipped the light switches off.

Instantly the room was cloaked in darkness.

With the lights out, she asked again. "How about now?"

Murmurs spread.

"Now we can't see a thing," one of the students said.

"Exactly," she replied.

A familiar voice responded. "I think I know the answer."

As Emily turned on the lights, the student who had mentioned the problem in the past raised a hand. "Amar?"

He pointed above him. "I'm not sure if this is it, but this fluorescent light above me has been out for several weeks."

Emily offered back a broad smile and stabbed a finger at him. "Ah, someone is paying attention. Come on down. It's yours." Heads turned as the Indian student made his way to the front, a look of disbelief spreading. He must have thought the hundred-dollar bill was a fake. It wasn't. As soon as he peeled it off the board, he held it up to the light to check.

"It's real," Emily said with a smirk.

The rest of the classroom roared with laughter as he made his way back to his seat.

"Thank you, Amar." Emily skirted around her desk and glanced at her notes. She lifted one of the papers and read from it, glancing up to gauge the reaction of her students. "A few years ago, there was an article published in *The New York Times* that stated five hundred species are likely to be extinct in the next two decades. That's twenty years from now. In your lifetime. That doesn't sound like a lot, right? I mean especially when there are estimated to be one to two million species of animals." She glanced down. "Scientists have reported that all large ocean fish could be gone by 2050 and that right now an estimated 70 percent of fish are already fully used, overused, or in a state of crisis." She paused. "Six years ago, *The Guardian* reported that the planet has already seen the number of wild animals drop by half in the past forty years. Four years ago, an article in *The Independent* mentioned that by 2020 that number will have gone up to 67 percent. So... birds, fish, reptiles, mammals, and other vertebrates, two-thirds of them are no longer with us." Emily glanced up. "Par for the course, right? I mean, some would say this is the natural decline that all species experience. The normal evolutionary life cycle. Or is it? Well, it appears it's not. Scientists are now saying that the loss of biodiversity is accelerating at an unnatural speed leading us towards another mass extinction. But is that the truth? Let's put this in perspective, shall we? Each year one in a million species expire naturally but what we are seeing is that this is now occurring one thousand times faster than it should be. Are you paying attention?" she asked. A few heads nodded. Emily knew she was dumping a lot on them and for many, it would go in one ear and out the other, but even if one person got it and took a step in the right direction, it would be worth it. "So, let's hear some of your theories on why this is happening."

She tossed it back to them, knowing that it would make them think.

"Deforestation." one student said.

She nodded. "We certainly have been expanding and encroaching."

"Disease?" someone asked.

She began to walk among them. "Sure. That is rampant today."

"Pollution."

Each of them began throwing out answers.

"Global warming."

She nodded.

"Animal testing."

"Overpopulation."

"Poaching."

"Overfishing."

"Globalization."

"Animal agriculture."

"Very good," she said. "So, what does this all amount to?"

There was no response for a moment then someone yelled, "We are screwing up the planet."

Laughter ensued.

Even though it wasn't a laughing matter, she couldn't help but stifle a chuckle and nod. "You are right. Sixty-five million years ago the dinosaurs were wiped out by what we believe was a giant meteor hitting the planet. But now what appears to be the culprit is us. We have become the asteroid. It's the reason why geologists are declaring a new epoch, called the Anthropocene — the human impact on the earth. Folks, we are at the tipping point. The alarm bells are ringing." She made a gesture as if she was ringing a bell and students smiled. She continued, "The trouble is not enough people know, not enough people care, but most of all, most are simply not paying attention... so the speed of extinction is only getting faster. How can that be?" She allowed another pause to let her previous words sink in. "Well, it's like that light above Amar's head. Until it directly impacts you, you probably won't notice. You certainly won't care. And you're bound to not pay attention. You'll think it's someone else's job to correct. Why? Because that's human nature." She strolled before them, catching the eye of Anna who was listening intently. "Of course, there are other factors — we're too busy with work, family, entertainment." She took a cell phone out of the hands of a student who was sending a text message. Emily put it down in front of him. "And distracted by cell phones."

Some laughed.

"Simply put, too many distractions keep us from realizing what is happening until it directly impacts us. But imagine if you will... imagine what would happen if tomorrow you woke up and all non-human species were gone."

"That would suck. Because I love my Big Mac." That garnered even more laughs from the class.

"Yes, Brad. The food chain would be impacted but that would be the least of your concerns. No, I want to widen your perspective here." She turned and pointed to the quote on the board. "John Muir said — 'When we try to pick out anything by itself, we find it is bound fast by a thousand invisible cords that cannot be broken, to everything else in the Universe.' What does this mean?" she asked, then waited for an answer.

Students stared at it, then at her.

"C'mon guys, it means that everything is connected. We don't own this planet, we share it. You remove one thing from this planet, another is affected. There is a domino effect that we cannot always see but everything on this planet is held together by thousands of invisible cords. Let me give you an example." Emily drew a breath and let it go, leaning back against her desk.

She glanced at her paperwork. "In 1958 the leader of the People's Republic of China decreed that all sparrows in the country were to be killed because they felt the birds were eating too much grain. They referred to them as pests. The result of killing them? A huge number of locusts appeared. The same ones that the sparrows would have eaten. And what did they do? The locusts ate all the crops. The very thing they were trying to avoid. Famine followed. Upwards of 55 million died of starvation. And it led to the worst ecological disaster in history. That was from 1959 to 1961. It was called the Great Chinese Famine. And that's just one example that demonstrates the domino effect of what can happen when we remove just one species out of the biosphere. It doesn't just affect crops; it affects every aspect of life including your ability to live. I could go on with the removal of wolves from Yellowstone National Park and how it led to an unbalanced ecosystem and then what happened when they reintroduced them in 1995 but I think you get the point." She paused. "Remember, folks, we don't own this planet, we share it."

She turned and set her paperwork down. Anna smiled at her. It was good to bring her along to let her see the impact that one person could have on others. Of course, Emily wasn't naïve enough to think that her words would change the world or even change those in the room. It was easier to get angry at the situation, and cast blame. That had always been the way of mankind. To blame others and hope that someone, anyone would correct what needed to be corrected. But there was another way.

"So, what's the answer... eating more plants?" a student muttered, slinking down into his seat, fist-pumping the guy beside him, and minimizing the whole talk. Emily understood that most would still think it was a joke. That's because they knew no better. They'd been conditioned to always have what they needed available. They were only seeing it from one angle but really, they weren't seeing it. That was because it wasn't having a large enough impact on them directly at that moment to cause alarm. But it would eventually.

Emily turned. "Well, the first step is to start paying attention to the world around you. You don't see what's happening, first and foremost because you're not paying attention, and the reason you aren't is that it might not be directly affecting your country, your state, your city, or you right now. However, the moment it does, trust me, you are going to pay attention, gripe, try to change the status quo, but by then it will be too late. Listen, everyone, this isn't just about your children or theirs in the long distant future. This is happening right now in our lifetime. In your lifetime. We need to realize the impact we are having negatively on this planet. Expecting others to fix it isn't going to fix it. Turning a blind eye won't either. Minimizing it all will only speed things up. This is something we all need to get on board before it's too late. Before the lights go out and the domino effect leads to the extinction of our species."

"So what can we do?" someone asked.

"Good question. Adopt sustainable practices, stop buying endangered animal products, fish and hunt at rates that allow for repopulating, protect habitats, reduce water pollution, use renewables as an alternative to fossil fuels, use solar panels and so on, and find other ways of slowing climate change. All of these are viable ways to help."

"It seems a little overwhelming," a student said.

"I agree. It is." She nodded. "But not as overwhelming as it will be if we don't do anything about it now. Start with one thing. Because trust me, at the rate non-human animal species are going extinct, it won't be what's on your plate that matters, it will be the impact it has on the plants, the planet, and human life." She paused for a moment. "That's it for today, folks. And remember..."

They all said it in unison before she could say it.

"We don't own this planet, we share it."

Emily smiled. "You got it!"

If that was the only thing they got, then it was worth it.

People shuffled out of their seats, slinging their bags over their shoulders and filling the aisle as they exited. Anna sat there sipping on her drink as Emily filled her briefcase with paperwork. Once all the students were out of the room and it was quiet, she turned and asked, "So? What did you think?"

Anna's eyes went wide. All theatrical, she said, "Mom, you gave away a hundred dollars."

Emily laughed as she collected her thermos and slung her bag over her shoulder. "That's all you took away from it?"

Anna slid out from her chair and made her way down. "I've heard you talk about the rest countless times, but a hundred dollars... why so much? You could have put five bucks up there and it would have had the same impact."

"Have you seen the price of coffee in the cafeteria?"

She laughed as she gave Anna a big hug.

"Ah, it was good to have you here, honey."

As they walked out, she asked again. "Did you enjoy today?"

"Yeah... though I would have enjoyed it more with that hundred-dollar bill in my pocket."

Emily ruffled Anna's hair as the two exited the lecture hall. "Anna, where's your travel case?"

"Oh, shoot. I left it. One second." She rushed back and returned a moment later.

"How many times have I told you..."

"I know. I'm sorry. It just slipped my mind."

"You can't let it."

Anna had type 1 diabetes and was dependent on insulin. Adjusting to the change had been a challenge. Like many families managing juvenile diabetes, they had to inject it fifteen to thirty minutes before meals, though the new insulin Lispro could be taken closer to the mealtime. Along with that, they had to remember to take the insulin travel cold case with her whenever they went anywhere, a task that had caused numerous U-turns in the road to go back and retrieve it. Fortunately, she was getting better at remembering but it was still worrying. If she ever went away with the school, would she forget to take it? Would a teacher forget to remind her? Without a dose, her blood sugar levels would rise, and if she didn't eat, or skipped meals, a concern that all parents had, her sugar levels could drop dangerously low. It felt like they were in a continuous balancing act that few understood.

It was late afternoon by the time they hit the road. On a good day with little to no traffic, it was a clear shot east on the NY-7 highway to their home in Eden Falls, Vermont. No more than an hour. In heavy traffic or bad weather, they could be looking at two hours but it was fine. Time with Anna was worth its weight in gold. Having just turned twelve, she was growing up fast and Emily knew these were the defining years. Days she wouldn't get back. That's why she made a point to always take time no matter how busy her schedule got, and there were plenty of days she was snowed under with papers to mark.

Emily had been working as a professor in the Department of Biological Sciences for the better part of six years. Six years of commuting five days a week. It wasn't bad but there were days in the winter that she'd considered landing a position closer to home.

She'd chewed over moving to the city, but what with Travis' job with Vermont Fish & Wildlife, and all their friends and family in Vermont, she'd opted to commute. While others might have griped about the additional hour on either end of the day, she saw it as a time to think, a moment of quiet when she could listen to podcasts, make phone calls, and learn a second language. That way when she was home, one hundred percent of her time could be funneled into the family.

A crack of thunder in the distance startled her.

Anna looked up from her iPhone in the passenger seat.

From the moment they'd stepped outside, dark clouds had rolled across the expansive grey sky threatening grim weather. Twenty minutes in, sheet lightning flashed and a severe storm squall with high winds pummeled the Lexus RX 350. The windshield wipers whipped back and forth in a hypnotic daze, clearing the deluge of rain that was bombarding the car.

Ahead, the traffic was moving without any problem. No accidents. That was a good thing. All it took was one and the whole stream of traffic could be backed up for miles. Emily glanced at the GPS to see the estimated time of arrival. She'd only taken her eyes off the road for a split second when it happened.

Thump.

It sounded like a brick hit them.

She didn't even see what it was that struck the windshield but her brain registered the hard impact as a dark foreign object cracked the glass. Somehow, she managed to stay in her lane until the next one hit, then another after that.

Birds.

Large, small, one after the other rained down from the sky like massive hailstones. Heavy, fast, and devastating. Countless. The sedan ahead of them swerved into the second lane, slamming into a pickup truck. A motorcycle crashed into an SUV. A tractor-trailer collided with a van then jack-knifed. There was no time to slam brakes on and it would have done little to help. Speeding vehicles of all types were barreling behind her. Like dominoes, one after the other, metal slammed together, sparks flew and flames burst from automobiles.

Everything happened so fast.

Brakes squealed. An eighteen-wheeler coming the other

way smashed into the median, tearing through it like butter, breaking off large chunks of concrete. Emily's eyes flashed as she jerked the wheel to avoid a black SUV. The slick road took control and with the brakes locked, the Lexus hydroplaned out of the lane. Anna screamed, her voice lost in the crunch of metal and the clatter of glass as another vehicle collided with theirs from behind, knocking it into the median and sending it into a dangerous flip.

The Lexus soared through the air and landed with a deafening thud.

2

An hour earlier
Eden Falls, Vermont

The two green-clad game wardens stared at the gruesome sight of a headless buck. It was a trophy kill. Nothing more. Not only had the animal been hunted out of season on posted private property without permission, but they hadn't even taken the body for meat. The poacher had shot it solely for the antlers and left the rest to rot.

It was a waste, a complete travesty, and yet it was just one among the many illegal activities Travis Young had come across in his eighteen years with the Fish & Wildlife Department. He was a fully certified law enforcement officer responsible for enforcement of state and federal laws, though he primarily focused on wildlife conservation and fish and game enforcement issues. Still, many considered the game wardens the Swiss Army knife of the state police. It wasn't just that they were trained at the police academy in Pittsford; they were often first on the scene after a 911 call in rural areas.

Like most unfamiliar with this line of work, he'd naively assumed before getting trained that his job would mostly involve tackling poachers shooting from the road and roaming the backcountry. Instead, he was thrown headfirst into the deep end, arresting people with a felony warrant; dealing with identity crimes, drunk drivers, drug cases, and domestics; aiding in search and rescues, and responding to attempted suicide.

But that wasn't an everyday event. Like most of his fellow game wardens, his interactions with the public were mostly making compliance checks for fishing and hunting licenses, protecting wild animals, and keeping the public safe.

Unpredictable best summed up the job.

It was never the same each day. That's what had kept it interesting all these years.

Travis removed his ball cap and wiped the sweat from his brow.

"Same ones as last year?" he asked.

Officer Hugh Richmond nodded. "That's what the owner thinks. Similar red truck. Although he didn't manage to get a license plate, he did nab a blurry snapshot of what looks like an F-150." Hugh rose from a crouched position beside the buck and showed him the photo the complainant had sent him. It wasn't good.

"I might be mistaken but..." Travis muttered, taking a look at it.

"You familiar with it?"

Travis stared off into the distance. "Ah, I'm sure there are lots of folks who have a red F-150 in Vermont... but I've only come across one in this district with a busted side mirror and it belongs to Don Chambers."

Don Chambers was a local whose family of avid hunters for the most part kept to themselves and followed rules, except for last year when they'd gotten into a heated dispute with a fellow game warden who seized his son's rifle and deer for recklessly shooting the animal within five hundred feet of a dwelling. The rules varied from state to state, and town to town; some knew, others didn't.

The crux of the matter was that they'd taken offense with the accusation leveled at them and felt their rights were being infringed. Although Don wasn't directly involved, he'd shown up in a drunken state to mouth off and get in the game warden's face.

When Travis arrived on scene as backup, he found the five of them shouting at the warden. And because Don had nothing to do with it, he didn't like being told to leave and had stood his ground, so Travis had warned him that if he wanted to press his luck, he'd end up in handcuffs. Fortunately, he and his relatives backed down. After explaining how things would go the next day, they wrapped it up for the evening. Still, word around town was the Chambers family wasn't happy about it. It had made him wonder if Don or one of his relatives had decided to clap back with this kill.

"I hope that's not the case," Hugh said.

Hugh thought it was just some youngsters, wet behind the ears and ignorant of the rules. He was confident about catching them this year even though the odds were low. Statistically, for every poacher they caught, ten got away. That was just the nature of the business they were in. Capturing poachers was a tough gig because it relied on so many factors. Timing. Assistance from the public. Proof like photos or video. Nowadays they were using all kinds of tech to improve those numbers — decoys, thermal imaging cameras, ballistic shockwave sensors, drones, and DNA analysis.

Although they frequently worked alone, Hugh had asked Travis to help him apprehend the group of poachers that had been spotlighting and shooting deer from the road on properties bordering the southern and northeast districts.

The crime was hardly unique. Despite the land being posted as a non-hunting area, the illegal behavior continued.

The trouble was by the time they got a call, the suspects were gone, leaving behind only the body and a distraught landowner. Poachers knew the odds of being caught were low. Most game wardens patrolled vast swaths of land and would often be found an hour deep in the backcountry when a call came in, making it almost impossible to respond in time. And that was both a hindrance and a danger when they needed backup.

While the vast majority of those they had contact with in the field were good, law-abiding hunters just looking to enjoy the natural resources — in many ways, his line of work was more dangerous than a regular peace officer because the people they encountered were usually armed. There was no telling what direction a contact might go in. "Always a few bad apples ruining it for the rest," Travis said. "I'll be interested to hear the excuse or lie."

"It's always the same. 'I didn't know.' Denial," Hugh said.

The problem was threefold. Ignorance, a refusal to abide by the laws, and a lack of landowners registering and posting their land each year. With roughly 85 percent of Vermont's land privately held, game wardens relied on owners' cooperation to manage the deer population, and because hunters had the constitutional right to hunt and fish on private properties unless they were enclosed, many didn't bother to read the rule book. However, that freedom to hunt came with stipulations. It relied on landowners posting clear signs to alert hunters to ask first or keep out, and it expected hunters to play by the book.

Most did.

The idiots were in the minority.

And, it wasn't like hunters could say they never saw a sign in Vermont, as posted signs were jokingly considered the state flower because you couldn't drive down a road without seeing them dotted four hundred feet apart.

Still, that didn't stop the bad element from doing whatever they pleased.

"I gather the owner will take the body?"

"Yeah, he's gone to get his truck."

If they had to put down lame animals found by the road, they had a list of people in the county that were willing to take the body away. That way the meat didn't go to waste but in this case, there was no need.

Hugh motioned with a nudge of the head. "I see you brought the film crew with you."

Travis cast a glance over his shoulder toward his mobile office, a Chevrolet Silverado 2500 pickup with an extended cab. It was black as they were slowly phasing out the green ones. On the driver's door was a bright yellow game warden emblem. Behind the glass, sitting in the passenger seat, was Lucas, Emily's ten-year-old son. He was pointing a cell phone at them. He had a curly mop of dark hair and bright round blue eyes, and a mischievous grin to top it off.

"Oh, yeah, it's Take Your Kid to Work Day," Travis responded.

"Huh. Kyle was good with that?"

"He doesn't know."

Hugh's eyes widened as he ran a hand over his head. "Best it stays that way." Hugh groaned. "What a day to bring the kid in."

Travis nodded. "Yeah, I figured it would be slow, he'd get to see a few simple compliance checks, ride up front, flip on the lights, and let the siren wail — not this." Travis didn't want Lucas to feel left out, especially since Anna had shown an interest to go with Emily, but at the same time, he didn't want to overstep the line. Travis had been seeing Emily for the better part of two years. While he adored her, it hadn't been an easy road. She was getting close to the tail end of a nasty divorce proceeding. The court had given her temporary custody of her kids and she was now locked in a battle with her ex. And, because of the fragility of the situation, the accusations leveled at Kyle, and the nature of his work, Emily had held off moving in with him until the divorce was finalized. Never having kids of his own, he'd soon grown attached to hers, and likewise, they'd warmed up to him once they saw how well he treated their mother.

"How's Emily?" Hugh asked.

"Oh, you know, as good as can be under the circumstances. Listen, I'd say you should swing by Don's place to deal with this but seeing how volatile he can get, I'll go with you. It could be that he has nothing to do with it but we'll see."

"You bringing him along? The situation could go south."

"Please. You give him too much credit. Don might have a mouth on him but he's not an idiot."

Travis returned to his truck. "Is the camera really necessary?" Travis said with a grin as he climbed back into the cab.

"It's footage, Travis. This stuff is gold."

"Yeah, well you'll have to delete that gold. We don't want the school or other parents calling us after you scare them to death with that gruesome sight."

"Did a black bear get it?"

"Oh no, it wasn't a bear," he said, distracted as he tapped an address into the GPS. Don lived outside of town, deep in a rural area where the roads were nothing more than uneven trails. "No, this was a different kind of predator."

"Why did they do it?"

"Because they're idiots," he replied, looking down checking his messages.

Lucas laughed. "No, they had to have a reason."

"Oh, they do."

"So, what is it?"

"That's what we hope to find out." He twisted in his seat. "Look, Lucas, some people in this world like to take more than they should."

"Why?"

He scoffed. "Greed. Ignorance. They like to test the boundaries. And some, well, they like to turn the tables on good people to get back at them. But that's why we're here."

"So, we're going to stop them?"

"That's the plan," he said, giving him a wink before he contacted dispatch and updated them on where they were heading next. The police radio in the center crackled. There were two microphones where the center console used to be.

"What are these for?" Lucas asked, pointing down at the console with his phone like some young indie filmmaker. Ever since he'd brought him out, he'd been a bundle of questions. Why, when, where, how? He was like a sponge trying to soak it all up to get an A in class.

Travis tapped the one microphone. "This is strictly for

Fish & Wildlife, the other goes to state, municipal, and the sheriff's department, but we also use that radio to contact other agencies. It's also how dispatch can get hold of us and we can monitor what's happening out there."

"Like what the bad guys are up to?"

He chuckled. "Yeah, something like that."

"And these?" Lucas asked, picking up binoculars. "These for bird watching?"

Travis smiled. "They're for everything. I don't have eyes like Superman but with these, it gets pretty darn close."

"And what about this?" Lucas asked, touching a third microphone.

"Pick it up and see."

Lucas snatched it up and pressed the button on the side and spoke into it. His voice boomed out of the PA system on top of the truck, startling Hugh who was bent over. "Oh, that's wild," Lucas said. Travis laughed, thinking that's not what Hugh was calling it under his breath.

"And these?"

"Blue lights, foghorn, sirens."

"Can I test them?"

"Later, kiddo." He tossed his citation book down. "I think poor old Hugh's heart might not handle it."

He stifled a laugh.

The truck's engine quietly rumbled as they waited for the landowner to come and collect the body before rolling out. Travis brought down his window to get some air. "When you find those responsible, are you going to shoot them?" Lucas asked, tapping Travis's Glock 23 tucked into his holster.

"I hope not."

A silver truck rolled up and the owner got out and waved.

Hugh approached him to update him on the investigation they would be conducting.

While they waited, Travis answered more questions, taking Lucas through what he wore, and what was on his duty belt. "We wear this in rain, snow, or sunshine. A bulletproof vest over the top of the shirt. This one is for the field." He tugged at his vest and readjusted his green baseball cap before going through each of the items on his belt. "Alright, we got an expandable baton, a radio that connects to the truck and dispatch, extra magazines, and OC spray."

"What do you use that for?"

"People. Dogs. I don't want to, but it's better than using this," he said, tapping the 40-caliber. He continued, "I carry two pairs of handcuffs and a Leatherman multi-tool." He thumbed over his shoulder. "Then in the back of my truck are my night-vision goggles, extra batteries, a Remington 12-gauge shotgun, and an M4."

When Hugh was ready, Travis told Lucas to buckle up and he peeled out following close behind.

Don Chambers lived on a property that butted up against the Green Mountain National Forest. It was a good thirty minutes of rough driving outside of Eden Falls.

Rural. Isolated. If it wasn't for previous run-ins with the man, he might have had his reservations about going out there, but that was all part of the job. His district meant patrolling Bennington County. And as it took him to fishing and hunting spots buried deep in God's country, that remoteness always carried an element of risk. "Here, you want some of this?" Travis said, handing Lucas some beef jerky. He tended to keep a few snacks like almonds and protein bars in the truck along with energy drinks and water because there was no telling how long he could be out on the road. He worked six days a week, most weekends, and a schedule that varied depending on investigations that could see him working into the night.

"So, you pretty much do what my dad does."

"Yeah, we're law enforcement officers."

"That's not what he calls you."

"Oh, no?" He waited for some of the nicknames to be tossed out except Lucas didn't. He paused and looked out the window as if he was about to say it but then opted not to. "Come on, spit it out."

"No, it's not nice."

"It's not like we haven't heard them before."

"He calls you a duck cop, Mr. Green Jeans, possum cop, and..."

He chuckled. "All right, all right, I get it." Their relationship with other law enforcement agencies was good and respect was mutual barring Kyle Mansfield.

But in all fairness, it wasn't just Kyle.

For many, there was a lack of understanding of what a game warden, otherwise known as a conservation officer, was. The uneducated might have thought they were state rangers, or better still busybodies trying to take all the fun out of hunting. But that wasn't it. While the primary responsibility was to protect wildlife and keep the public safe, they were also commissioned alongside the state highway patrol. They were federal officers able to enforce federal laws and even had more power than local police when it came to searches. They could go into any open field on private land without a warrant and without producing just cause to investigate poaching and other crimes. When they weren't hunting for poachers, they were often collecting gossip at the general store, hiding in roadside ditches, setting up decoys, issuing tickets, assisting with search and rescue, checking licenses, issuing citations, and writing courtesy notices.

Focusing on fishing, trapping, hunting, and boating, they were a unit that also could plug into any environment and respond to multiple calls as a force multiplier.

Simply put, when someone phoned 911 about a domestic, a felony in progress, attempted suicide, or even a murder investigation, it very well could be one of them arriving on scene.

Travis eased off the gas as they rolled over the bumpy ground that led up to a mobile home nestled in the woodland. It was a ramshackle abode in desperate need of repair or better still, being demolished. Garbage and all manner of weathered items dotted the front yard including a couple of ATVs with torn seating, a rusty swing set, a BBQ that had seen better days, water barrels, buckets, paint cans, a child's bike, random pieces of drywall, and even an air conditioner. How anyone lived like this was beyond him but rural living presented all manner of interesting people.

Don had either heard or seen them coming on surveillance as he was there to greet them when they pulled in. A matted mutt trotted over to check them out as Travis got out. "Stay here," he said to Lucas. "Keep your head down. Okay?"

"Got it."

He slammed the door shut and rested one hand on his service weapon.

"I hope you got a warrant," Don said, making his way down off the porch. He was in his early sixties, slightly overweight with a gut peeking out from beneath an off-white T-shirt partially hidden by a camo jacket. He had a five o'clock shadow and greying hair sticking out the back and sides of his hunting baseball cap.

Hugh hung back as the cover officer while he made contact.

"Don, we're not here to cause trouble. We just have a few questions for you."

"Uh-huh."

"It's about bucks that have been killed on a property without permission to hunt."

"Don't know nothing about that."

"There have been three beheaded in the past two months. You heard anything?"

Rumors circulated pretty fast.

"Nope. Besides, it's out of season. That would be breaking the law, now wouldn't it, officer?" He had this smug grin on his face.

Travis nodded, his gaze roaming. "Where's your F-150?"

"What's it to you?"

Hugh approached and handed Travis his phone so he could show him. Travis gave Don a good look at it. "That wouldn't be yours, would it?"

"You think that's mine? Hell, I've seen clearer shots of Sasquatch."

Don's eyes bounced between them. He swallowed hard. He had this nervous twitch.

"I admit it's not clear, but the missing side mirror. The same one you were asked to get repaired and you never did. Come on, Don. Where's the truck?"

"It's with my son and cousin."

"Nate?"

"Uh-huh," he replied, nodding and leaning up against the

porch railing. He wasn't in the best of shape and just talking to them was making him huff and puff.

"You got a number for him?"

There was some hesitation but if he was telling the truth and he wasn't involved and his son and cousin were behind it, he knew it would come back to bite him in the ass especially if they were using his truck. He nodded. Travis had Done phone the number to check if Nate was around. He didn't want to get there only to have Don give them the heads-up so they could dispose of any evidence.

He shrugged. "He's not answering."

Don handed his phone over for him to check. Travis tried the number and heard it go to voicemail.

"How about an address?" Travis asked.

Don reeled it off. It was some shack not far away. A few miles down the road. They hopped back in their vehicles and tore out of there. Hugh hoped to keep the line tied up by trying the number as they barreled down a heavily wooded trail toward Nate's property. It was possible that Don was lying and he would try to give him the heads-up. People wanting to stay out of trouble often did, but Travis could tell from his facial expression that even he was surprised. Maybe Nate had kept his pops out of the loop.

They veered onto a property with a trailer and a weathered barn. His son had about the same enthusiasm and pride in keeping the land tidy as his father did. There were a couple of dirt bikes, three old beat-up cars, and an ATV with a fully dressed mannequin perched on it which looked strange. Nearby was a ripped tent, empty beer bottles dotting the brush, and dented metal targets for shooting. While there was no truck outside, they did find two deer heads recently skinned around the back.

"Bingo," Hugh said.

Travis knocked on the door and stepped back, crushing a beer can beneath his boot.

"Game warden!" He listened. Nothing. He pounded the door with a fist. "Game warden!" No one answered. There was a chance the son and cousin were inside. Travis sidled up to the weathered barn and peered in through one of the dusty windows.

Inside he saw something even more concerning — drug paraphernalia and a lot of it. It looked like they had a mini meth lab. He notified Hugh and immediately had him get in contact with state troopers to back them up.

This was probably the worst day he could have brought Lucas out.

If Nate was somewhere inside and he felt trapped like a caged animal, there was no telling how he would respond. And with the location being so rural and far out, they were going to have to wait another thirty minutes for backup.

When state finally arrived, the tension went from zero to ten quick, and not because of the suspect. Trailing behind the trooper was Sheriff's Deputy Kyle Mansfield, Lucas' father. As soon as they made eye contact, Kyle made a beeline for Travis. Their interactions since Kyle got wind of Emily's involvement with Travis had been few and far between. Although communication between Kyle and Emily was meant to go through lawyers, he felt his position in law enforcement allowed him to do whatever the hell he liked.

The few times they'd exchanged words, Travis had gotten a sense that he didn't like him but that was to be expected.

Here was a guy he'd known through situations like this now dating his ex. As the divorce wasn't finalized due to him being an ass, and the circumstances surrounding their separation, it was natural to think that Travis had been having an affair with Emily while the two of them were together but that wasn't the case. She'd only contacted him after leaving Kyle.

"Kyle."

"Travis," he said with a nod before looking into the cab where Lucas was peering out. "Why's he here?"

"Because he is."

"Are you being smart with me?"

"Relax. It's Take Your Kid to Work Day."

Kyle's brows went up. "Oh, really. So, he's your kid now?"

"Let's not do this in front of him, Kyle." Travis looked back at Lucas who had shrunken down in his seat. Although Emily said that Kyle had never hit them, the fear was evident. Abrupt, brazen, a hard drinker known for losing his cool, his reputation preceded him and not just because Emily had said it. Folks in town knew. He was the kind of man that gave the badge a bad name. Ego-driven, Emily said. He liked people to know he was a cop, that he carried some power that he could lord over others.

Kyle ignored Travis and rapped on the window with his knuckles. "Hey, Lucas." He rapped again. "Son, why don't you..."

"You mind not doing that," Travis said, cutting him off.

"Oh, settle down, there's no mark."

"I wasn't referring to that."

Kyle shot him a sideways glance. "Do we have a problem?"

"You know what the court said."

Kyle narrowed his eyes. "Yeah, until it's finalized, he's my kid, and Emily's still my wife."

"She stopped being your wife the day you raised a hand to her."

He chuckled, looking away. "Of course she did. I expect Emily's told you I beat the kids too," he said without looking at him. He kept his eyes on Lucas. "You know, Travis, when all is said and done, you're going to feel really stupid that you were reeled into her lies."

"Yeah, well until then it's best you keep your distance and focus on why you're here."

"Is that an order or a threat?" he asked. "Cause a person might get the wrong idea."

While their interaction was occurring, Hugh and the state trooper were peering through the window of the barn. Hugh was on the phone. The two of them caught wind of Kyle raising his voice and squaring up to Travis. Hugh jogged over to intervene. "Guys, how about you save this until after your shift? Nate just answered his phone, he's on his way back. Seems Don got hold of him. Once he arrives, he's permitting us to search the building and his father's truck. Denies everything."

"And the lab?"

"He said he wasn't aware of it. That he's been renting out this place to his cousin."

Travis shifted uncomfortably from one foot to the next as Kyle eyed him. "Convenient. And let me guess, this cousin is also responsible for the two skinned deer heads around back?"

"He didn't say but..."

Just as Hugh was spitting out the words, a large crow hit the windshield of the state cop's cruiser, cracking it with a startling thud. Another followed, then three more. Travis' eyes widened, as all around birds began raining down out of the sky. The three of them darted for the cover of the old carport and looked on in shock as birds of every size and type pummeled the earth.

3

Albany, New York

It was a strange form of hell that made her question whether she was alive or dead. She blinked hard, pain coursed through her body, a mix of aches and sharp spikes of agony as if her collarbone was snapped. The truth was, it was a seat belt biting into her flesh, holding her in place as she hung suspended upside down in the passenger seat.

Anna's mind tried to make sense of the madness.

Flashes of light.

Screams.

Car horns blaring.

People running by her.

And the sight of birds. Everywhere. A bloody mess of feathers covering the asphalt outside. She managed to force out the word "help" but it was expelled as nothing more than a muffled cry. Quickly her mind pieced together what had happened.

Traveling in the car with her mother.

A conversation about what they would eat that evening.

Then, birds raining down, several hitting the windshield like black bullets.

Brakes screeched, cars swerved, and then a jolt so hard from behind that it thrust them forward into the tangled web of metal clogging up the four-lane highway out of the city. She didn't remember blacking out but soaring through the air upside down as the SUV twisted. How was she still alive?

"Mom?"

No answer.

Anna's face was mashed against the ceiling of the vehicle. She could feel warm liquid on her face and the smell of iron. Blood. She was bleeding. Instinctively, Anna reached around to unbuckle herself, to free her body from the harsh constraints that were slicing into her skin.

Click.

As soon as the belt was released, the rest of her body crumpled, curling around.

Another jolt of pain radiated through her.

Had she broken any bones?

Lucas had broken his arm when he was nine, falling out of a tree. She remembered the gross shape, how it bent back in a way that it shouldn't. And the screams. Oh, she couldn't get that out of her mind for days.

No. She hadn't broken anything otherwise she would be in more pain.

Twisting against the vehicle's ceiling, she glanced at her

mother who was still upside down, her long auburn hair hanging loosely. "Mom? Hey," she said, reaching to touch her face. She couldn't hear any breathing. It was a jumbled mess. Her mother's briefcase from the back seat had opened, sending papers everywhere. The windshield had smashed and the dashboard was crumpled. The fact that she'd managed to survive was a miracle in itself.

"Mom!"

Fear rushed up her throat, choking her as tears emptied and rolled down her cheeks. The thought that her mother was dead almost paralyzed her mind from thinking straight. She'd never been in a car accident. She'd never been alone in a city. Outside, she could hear only chaos. Yelling. Screams. And she smelled fumes and smoke. Disoriented, she looked out through smoke drifting across the highway and saw the face of a solitary man, a businessman who had been ejected out of his windshield and had landed nearby. His eyes were still open, his mouth agape.

"Help!" she yelled but her voice was lost in the unfolding hell that had befallen the city. She didn't even think about what had caused the birds to fall. All that went through her mind was fear. Pure terror.

Anna shook her mother, hoping that might wake her. She leaned in close, trying to hear her breathing but it was too loud outside, and the way her mother's clothes were sitting on her body she couldn't see if her stomach was rising or falling.

Pushing through the fog of panic, one clear thought persisted.

Phone.

My phone.

Anna dug into her jacket pocket and retrieved her iPhone.

Without a moment of hesitation, she swiped up, hit the emergency button, and dialed 911.

"C'mon, c'mon," she muttered, looking at her mother.

Tears continued to roll down her cheeks.

All she got was a busy signal.

"No. No. No!" she repeated, trying again.

Same thing. Nothing but a busy line.

How many other people were calling for emergency services?

She looked out at the birds dotted throughout the highway. How many had fallen? Was it only here? Or was this happening all over the country? No, it was impossible. But that would explain why the phone lines were tied up. If it had occurred everywhere, there would be crashes on every back road and highway. Realistically, how many calls could dispatch handle at once? Even a backup call center wasn't made for this. Anna kept trying as she turned her body in the mess of papers that littered the inside like large confetti. A hard wind blew in, bringing with it the rain.

She shivered ever so slightly, hands trembling.

"Mom, please wake up. Please."

She shook her again but got no response. One side of her mother's face was covered in blood. After multiple attempts at trying 911, she did the only thing she could do, she dialed Travis' number but his phone was busy.

The next call she made was to Lucas.

A few seconds of panic because he didn't answer and then relief flooded her chest as she heard his voice. "Hello?"

"Lucas."

"Anna, the birds have..."

"Lucas, listen to me; I need you to get Travis. We've... been..."

She couldn't get the words out fast enough. Like a sinking person desperately reaching for a lifebuoy ring, and struggling to tread water, she struggled to connect words. "... in an accident. Mom's not waking up."

"What?"

"Get Travis."

She heard him fumble with his phone and then a window going down before hearing him bellow, "TRAVIS! QUICK!"

Breathing hard she looked at her mother again and gave her another shake. No response. *Please don't be dead. Please.* All the things she'd never told her mother. All the things she wouldn't get to experience came bubbling to the surface of her mind. A second later, she heard his voice.

"Anna. It's Travis."

Hearing his voice just made her release all her anguish. Tears poured out as she tried to tell him about what had happened, the birds, the crash, her mother not waking up, but it all came out as a jumbled blubbering mess of snot and tears.

"Hey, hey, calm down, take a breath. Listen to me. Take a breath. It's going to be okay. Now tell me what's happened? Where's your mom?"

Her chest rose and fell fast as she sucked in air and tried to get a grip. Finally able to speak, she brought him up to speed. "I don't know what to do. I tried calling 911 but no one is answering and mom is..."

"All right, listen to me. First things first. Can you see any flames?"

"Yes, but it's not coming from this car."

"What about smoke?"

"There's smoke coming out of the engine."

"Any liquid?"

"I can't see. I'm stuck in this small space and there is glass everywhere."

"Is your mom breathing?"

"I can't hear. It's too loud." She had a finger stuck in one ear and the phone pressed against the other. The loud blaring of horns made it almost impossible to hear Travis.

"All right, here's what I want you to do. Put two fingers on the side of your mother's neck. Search for her artery. I want you to feel for a pulse. Can you do that?"

"Two fingers. Yep," she said. She hadn't even thought about doing that as panic had taken over, and she just assumed her mother was dead. Anna shifted and got as close as she could beneath her mother and reached through the tangled mass of hair to touch the side of her neck.

"Anna. How are we doing?'

"One second."

It took a moment to find it but when she did, a sense of relief washed over her. "I've got it. It's strong."

"She's alive. That's what matters. Is she breathing?"

She got close and could feel wisps of air pushing past her bloodied lips. "Yeah, but there's so much blood."

"All right. Good girl. Can you unbuckle your mother?"

Anna fumbled with the seat belt buckle but unlike hers, it was crumpled, and attempts to press the button were met with resistance. She pulled hard but that did nothing.

"Any luck?" he probed.

"No. It's stuck."

"Okay. Look, the emergency lines are tied up right now, there's a chance the vehicle you're in could be leaking gasoline. I need you to climb out, find someone to help get your mother out."

"But..."

"Anna. Just do as I say."

"I'm scared."

"I know you are, honey, but we need to get your mother away from that car."

"All right." Twisting in the confined space, Anna slid toward the passenger side window where the glass was now gone. A few jagged pieces stuck into her as she pulled herself out and stumbled to her feet. That's when she felt more pain. As soon as her arm hung down, she noticed one of her fingernails was torn off, and her elbow was radiating an enormous amount of pain. Groaning, she looked through the smoke coming from multiple vehicles and assessed the situation.

She'd seen traffic accidents before on the news and they usually only involved two or three vehicles. This was far worse. For as far as the eye could see, vehicles were in various states of trouble. Some had left the road and were in the ditch, others flipped, some had been sheared in half.

There were bodies everywhere.

And even more birds.

"What do you see, Anna?"

She struggled to put it into words. "Death. Collisions..." Her voice trailed off.

"I want you to focus on one person. Find one person. An adult that's nearby and go and ask them for help."

"All right," she said, taking a few steps forward. She might not have broken a bone, but it was possible she'd sprained her ankle as with each step she felt a spike of agony. Tears continued to flow down her cheeks as she zeroed in on a black woman who had her back to Anna. She was kneeling beside a vehicle, rocking back and forth. The doors were open, there was a male slumped over the wheel.

"Do you see anyone?" Travis asked.

"Yeah." She shuffled over to the woman. "Hello. I need some help. Can you..."

As the words came out, the woman turned her head and Anna noticed she was holding a limp baby in her arms. Just one look at what was left of the child's face and it was clear it was dead. The woman looked in shock. Her eyes were wide. Tears streaking her face. Anna turned away. "I'm sorry. I'm sorry," she said as she continued her search. Many were slumped over steering wheels in their cars. Some were outside performing CPR on loved ones, while others were huddled with their children, ignoring her pleas. Everyone was too distraught or in shock to notice her small cry for help.

She turned at the sound of an engine. A black truck came barreling toward her in the emergency lane. At first, she thought it was emergency services but it shot by almost hitting her. At the last second, the driver slammed the brakes on, and the rear lights blinked red. Several people approached the truck asking for help but were dismissed by the driver and passenger as they got out.

It was a male and female.

Both in their forties at a rough guess.

He was wearing an NYC baseball cap, a white T-shirt, black jeans, and work boots. The woman had on a pair of blue shorts, a big brown buckle belt, and a tight green tank top that made her large breasts spill out.

"Please. Can you help? It's an emergency. My mother is in..." Anna trailed off as she turned and pointed to their vehicle.

"Anna. Hey, I'm losing you..." Travis said as the line crackled. "Have you found someone?" She could hear his voice over the speaker but was too busy asking the occupants of the truck for help as she shuffled toward them.

The woman, who had raggedy long hair that extended past her shoulders, gave a strained smile as she bent at the waist, placed her hands on her knees, and looked toward their vehicle. "Hey darlin', are you okay?"

"I need help. My mother is in our car and..."

"That one?" she pointed.

"Yeah. I need to get her out. She's trapped inside and..."

"Anna!" Travis yelled but she was too distracted.

Right then a flame burst to life on the Lexus.

SECONDS EARLIER, Emily roused from her unconscious state. She was disoriented and overwhelmed as noise and images attacked her senses from every angle. In the mix of chaos, pain gripped her, holding her tight, driving spikes of agony up her thigh to her brain, the body's warning system alerting her to impending danger.

Like watching a movie play, the previous moments came rushing at her, too fast, too many, too frightening.

Rocked to the core, she could taste blood in her mouth.

How injured was she?

Emily spat and coughed hard, her lungs screaming in protest as smoke flooded through the windshield trying to suffocate her. She could hear the crackle of flames but was unable to tell if it was her vehicle or another.

She squinted. "Anna?"

That was the first thought that went through her mind.

Her daughter. Was she alive? Where was she?

Emily twisted in her seat as much as the belt would allow

toward the passenger side. It was empty. There was a trail of blood outside. Had she been ejected from her seat? The sight of a dead man nearby spiked anxiety. Every movement made her cry in agony as she tried to unbuckle.

Pressing the red button did nothing.

Stuck. She tugged it. Pressed again and then looked out the window.

Squinting, she caught sight of Anna, that jean jacket they'd bought for her birthday a few months ago. The red Converse sneakers, black T-shirt, and cream-colored pants. "Anna," she said, summoning her loudest cry but she couldn't hear her. A black truck burst past, almost hitting Anna. She cried out to her but the smoke was getting worse and making her breathing labored. As she continued to try and unbuckle the seat belt, she watched as the occupants got out of the truck and Anna pointed her way.

Good girl. Smart.

Get help.

A woman approached Anna and bent at the waist talking to her. They looked toward the Lexus. *All right. All right. That's good. They'd get her out. Then she could take stock of the situation. Get an ambulance and...*

It happened at such an astonishing speed. Anna let out a terrifying scream that was quickly muffled as the meaty hand of a stranger covered her nose and mouth with a handkerchief and hauled her back toward the truck. The woman took hold of her legs and...

A cell phone dropped out of Anna's hand, hitting the ground and bouncing.

Fear closed her throat, almost too tight to scream.

"ANNA! NO... NO... NO!"

All Emily could do was watch in horror as her daughter

tried to fight but her body was lifted into the air from behind and her legs flailed aimlessly in the open space.

There was so much noise from the blaring of horns and so much chaos, the few people she could see weren't paying attention, and even if they did see, would they even know she was being abducted?

4

Vermont

"Anna!" Travis yelled. Confusion set in hard and fast. Not only was he wrestling with a mysterious event that had caused birds to rain down from on high but all that was overshadowed by the news of the accident.

For a second, he thought Anna had found help.

He'd heard someone talking to her, then the line broke up and the last he heard was a scream. Instantly after the line went dead, he'd tried phoning back but it just went to voicemail. In the commotion of him yelling, Kyle had overheard and was standing beside him trying to get an answer.

"What's happened?"

"Yeah, there's been an accident," he said, trying to phone Emily's number. It too went to voicemail. He hung up and waited, hoping Anna would phone back. All the while Hugh and the state trooper were trying to make sense of the unnatural event. Hugh had donned a pair of blue latex gloves and was crouched examining one of two crows that had put a large dent in the hood of his truck.

"Is she alive?" Kyle asked.

"As far as I know, but Anna..." he trailed off, his mind trying to stay calm and think through the situation.

Kyle didn't wait for more information, he walked off, getting on the phone trying to contact his daughter. It was no use. No one answered. Travis hurried over to his truck and opened the driver's side door. There was no time to get Lucas out when the birds dropped but he wanted to check that he was okay. "You okay, kiddo?"

"What's going on, Travis? Is my mom dead?"

"No, she's alive. I'm just waiting to see if Anna will call back. Your dad's trying to get through to her." He didn't want to tell him that the call dropped.

"What do you make of it?" the trooper asked, appearing at his side. "You think they were hit by a plane?"

"No, birds came down in Albany, too," Travis said, relaying the information Anna had given. He looked to Hugh. Hugh had been a game warden for far longer than him. He'd seen all manner of mysterious animal deaths.

"What have we got, Hugh?"

He grimaced, pulling off his baseball cap and scratching the back of his head. "Beats me." He looked up into the sky as a light rain fell. "It reminds me of what happened in Arkansas back in January last year. Caused several accidents."

"It happened there?"

"Yeah," he replied. "The same thing happened a year before that. But only over the city of Beebe and within one square mile. Over 5,000 red-wing blackbirds, European starlings, brown-headed cowbirds, and grackles. They landed on roads, roofs, front lawns, backyards, and crashed into cars."

"And what did they say caused that?" the trooper asked.

He shrugged. "Arkansas Game and Fish took away some of the birds for testing. No one was able to give a definite answer. Theories were put out that the birds were spooked by loud explosions from fireworks as it happened both times when it was New Year's Eve."

"Yeah, well, it's April," Trooper Callaway said. "And this is Vermont. But you said it's happened in Albany?" he asked, turning to Travis.

He nodded. "That's not all, 911 lines are tied up," Travis said.

"Of course they are," Kyle said waltzing over, shaking his head in frustration. "I can't get through to Anna or Emily. What was the last thing she said to you?" Kyle asked in a demanding tone, getting up in Travis' face. He took a few steps back and scowled before answering.

"That birds fell and they were involved in a collision. The vehicle flipped and Emily was trapped inside, unconscious."

"And what did you tell Anna?"

"To get help because she'd already tried 911."

"And Emily?"

"I just told you. She's alive but..."

"But what?"

He sighed. "Anna was getting help then I heard a scream and..."

"And what?"

"And that's it."

"She didn't say anything else?"

"No." He put a hand out. "You want to back up."

"She must have said something to you."

"That was it."

"Hey, Kyle, steady man," Hugh said, getting between them as the situation escalated. The two of them hadn't seen eye to eye since news spread of him and Emily. The few times Kyle had shown up at incidents, they'd endured each other, keeping words to a minimum, but with the divorce proceedings nearing the finish line, his disdain for Travis grew stronger.

"Stay out of it, Hugh."

Trooper Callaway put a hand on Kyle's shoulder and he shrugged it off, walking around the truck to speak with Lucas. No doubt to pester him for details. "Anyway," Hugh added. "The preliminary lab results from the Arkansas Livestock and Poultry Commission said that the birds had died from acute physical trauma. Whether that was from hitting the ground or being hit in the air is unknown. However, there were no indications of disease. They were running tests for toxic chemicals but nothing came back on that so the AFGC said that they think the birds were startled by the fireworks and ended up hitting houses and trees and so forth. It's not the first time it's happened. A few days before that 85,000 fish were found dead along the Arkansas River."

The trooper shook his head. "Geesh."

"They were pulling them out of the water for up to twenty miles. But in that case, it was a disease that was the culprit."

"You think this could be a disease?"

"No idea. But if it's happened in Albany, who knows."

Travis tried Anna's number again while Hugh was talking but just got the voicemail. He brought up the internet and did a quick news search. That's when he got the first inkling of the scope of what had happened. Every media outlet across the country was reporting the same thing. Birds falling dead from the sky in some mysterious event. He extended his search to outside of the country and his jaw dropped.

Australia.

England.

France.

Africa.

Russia.

China.

The list continued, this wasn't an isolated event, it was global. An inexplicable mass die-off around the world and so far, no one could offer an answer. "Hey guys..." he turned his phone around and showed them. They huddled, scanning the articles, perplexed. Kyle noticed and made his way over.

"So, what is it?"

"I don't know," Travis said.

Kyle frowned. "But aren't you meant to know? Aren't you the go-to for these kinds of things?'

Travis snorted, shaking his head. "Man, you are something else."

Hugh answered him instead. "There's a different agency that handles the testing."

"But you said this has happened before."

"In isolated areas. Not across the globe."

EMILY SCREAMED until she almost lost her voice. She'd watched in horror as the truck did a U-turn and tore away taking Anna with them. She'd made a mental note to catch the license plate number. She kept repeating it over and over out of fear that she would forget.

234TUB

234TUB

234TUB

Her heart pounded in her chest as she frantically tried to get free from the seat belt. As more smoke poured in, an explosion occurred above at the front of the car.

Desperate, and choking on smoke, she knew the clock was ticking. If she didn't get out now, she'd burn to death or die of smoke inhalation.

But all attempts to get the buckle loose failed.

It was crumpled, jammed. Emily continued to scream. Someone had to hear her. But she didn't realize the full extent of what the world was going through at that moment. Shock, confusion, fear, death, it was all blended and she wasn't the only one trapped in a vehicle.

Her eyes scanned for something, anything that she could use to cut her way out. That's when she saw something that rocked her to the core. As if her stress couldn't get any higher, it now skyrocketed. There, nearby on the ceiling, was Anna's insulin travel case.

"Oh, God. No."

The harsh reality of the situation weighed down on her like a ton of bricks. Without insulin, her blood sugar levels would rise. Too much sugar in the blood would affect her organs. On a good day, how she felt depended heavily on what she ate and drank. It was one hell of a balancing act. Without it, hyperglycemia would lead to increased thirst, headaches, tiredness, and then all manner of problems. If she kept eating normally but didn't have the dose, she could enter ketoacidosis and that would lead to a diabetic coma and death.

Upside down, Emily scanned the glass. She removed the

thin green scarf around her neck, wound it around her hand, and then scooped up the largest piece she could find.

As she was hacking into the seat belt, a thought dawned on her.

Her phone. It had been plugged in at the time. Where was it now?

Even though it was out of sight, out of reach, she could...

"Hey Siri!" she yelled, hoping it would hear her. The damn thing had a mind of its own. There were times she had to bellow at the top of her voice to get it to respond and then other times she could be whispering and it would hear. Three times she called out to it and then it responded.

"Hello, Emily."

"Phone 911." She figured if she could give them the details of the black truck and the license plate, a cop might be able to spot it. Again, unaware of what was taking place, she did the only thing she knew to do.

"Hmm... I don't have an answer for that. Is there something else I can help with?"

"No, don't do this to me now."

"I don't understand what you said."

"Hey, Siri! Stop!"

"Okay."

She cursed. Damn technology. There were days it worked like magic and times it was more of an annoyance. She repeated the request and this time it understood and dialed.

When she heard the busy signal her stomach sank.

Emily scanned the scene outside as she continued to cough. She tried again to get through to 911 but got the same response. Four times. Four damn times she tried without luck.

Had the system shut down?

Long wait times would cause delays.

Continuing to hack away at the seat belt, she managed to slice through the strap across her chest and her body felt instant relief. But she was still suspended, held in place by the strap across her waist.

Her cough worsened. Her eyes stung.

Desperation took hold as she began to feel the heat of the flames.

Could no one see or hear her? She didn't stop yelling for help but no one came. Maybe they couldn't see her behind the wall of black smoke. She'd have to be her salvation. As she worked hard at the belt, the glass shard cut through the thin scarf, slicing into her hand. She winced in pain but didn't let up. A moment of agony to avoid death. Her brain pushed the pain from her mind, even the injuries she'd endured, as adrenaline flooded her system and took over.

Just as she was getting through the last part, a face appeared at her window, a woman no older than twenty. "Here, give me your hand."

Finally. Someone had heard.

"I'm still tied in. I'm nearly through," Emily said. A few more slashes and she was released from her restraint. Her body buckled and excruciating pain went through her as the young woman took hold of her wrists and pulled her out of the driver's side window, coughing and spluttering.

"I need my kid's insulin. It's..."

It was too late, flames blasted in, consuming the passenger side seat, and producing even more toxic smoke. It billowed out, black and thick.

Another person nearby, a male, Hispanic, hurried over to help. He heard her yelling about a blue insulin pack and quickly ran around and in some feat of bravery reached inside and pulled the pack out.

Within seconds the woman had her away from the vehicle. All of them were coughing badly. "Here you go. Is your kid around?"

"No. She's gone."

The male didn't stick around to ask where but jogged to the next vehicle, determined to help others. Had she not been in pain, or thinking about Anna, she might have thanked him.

"Your kid?" the woman asked. "Where is she?"

"She..." she tried to spit out the words but a coughing fit prevented them from coming out.

"Look, I need to help others. Are you good?"

Emily nodded, giving her a thumbs-up.

She was anything but good, her body was screaming in pain, but it was clear after being pulled from the Lexus that there were countless people in situations just like her, and others too distraught and in shock to focus on one person. The woman took off, leaving her propped up against the rear wheel of a truck.

She began to assess her injuries.

Emily could tell without even looking that her leg was broken. The pain was excruciating. She hoisted up her pant leg, gritting her teeth with each pull, to reveal the grotesquely deformed leg that was a deep purple. It was swollen and felt tight, a result of internal bleeding. Thankfully the bone hadn't broken through the skin.

On top of that, Emily was sure a rib was broken too as each inhale was labored and painfully sharp. She gripped her ribs and slowed her breathing so she could focus on what to do next.

Without her phone, her eyes roamed for the one Anna had dropped.

It was at least a good twenty feet away on the four-lane highway. Had she remembered, she would have asked the woman to get the phone or make a call for her.

Summoning the strength to push through spikes of pain, Emily dropped onto her side and grimaced as she pulled herself across the road toward the phone. Now that she was out of the vehicle and her adrenaline had dropped, her nerve endings were alive and she could feel every ounce of pain.

It took her a few minutes to reach the light pink phone.

Her hand clamped onto it tightly. The corner of the screen was slightly cracked but the hard outer case had protected the rest. Laying there in the emergency lane, she shuffled herself out of the way just in case another vehicle came along.

Breathing hard, Emily leaned back against the truck and tapped in the passcode.

The agreement she'd made with her daughter was she could have a phone on the condition that Emily was allowed to check it from time to time. All of which meant having no passcode to get into it. She had an open policy in the house on all computers. Anna was only twelve after all, and she knew how mean some kids could be on social media; then there was chatting with strangers and all manner of trouble. She wasn't going to have any secrets. Emily brought up her contacts and tapped Travis.

He picked up immediately. "Anna?"

"No, it's me."

"Emily?"

Out of breath, she pushed the words out. "They took her, Travis. They took her."

"What? Who?"

She struggled to catch her breath. "I don't know. A man and woman. They pulled her into a black Ram 3500. I got the license plate. It's..." she began reeling it off when Travis stopped her.

"Emily. Hey. Hold on. Are you okay?"

What was happening with Anna was out of their control, at least initially. Naturally, his fear for her bubbled to the surface. "Yeah. Don't worry about me. Listen, Travis. I think my leg is broken, I... I need you to find her."

"Find her? I've been trying to get through to emergency services in Albany but no one is responding. Look, where are you? I'll come and—"

"No. No. LISTEN!" Her voice cut through his.

Her mothering instincts kicked in, loud and furious, like a mother bear eager to get her cub back. "There's no time. She could be miles from here by the time you get to me. I'll be fine. Can't you get dispatch to connect with Albany through your radio? It's a different system from the 911 emergency, isn't it? Can't you alert them? Get them to put out an Amber Alert. We need cops looking for that truck. We need..."

"Emily, stop. Take a breath. Listen to me, everything is tied up right now. That includes our dispatch and other agencies."

"But. I thought—"

"Look, even if I can eventually make contact with Albany State Police, this thing is bigger than Albany. Something massive has happened across the country, hell, even the globe. And right now, the main roads are clogged with accidents. So, it wouldn't matter. Emergency services will be having a hard enough time trying to reach everyone. That's why the lines are tied up. Everyone is calling. There will be delays. So even if we could get hold of someone, it could take days to find that vehicle. It would be like trying to find a needle in a haystack right now." He paused and took a breath.

Silence stretched between them.

She was gutted. This wasn't happening. Not to her daughter. Not now.

Travis continued, "And besides, whoever took Anna probably stole the truck. We don't even know where they are or where they're going."

Emily looked down at Anna's iPhone, her eyes roaming the apps.

Her gaze zeroing in on one.

Then she remembered.

"I do," she said.

5

Vermont

"Would you shut up!" Travis yelled at Kyle who was demanding to speak with Emily. Travis got into his truck, ready to leave, but noticed he couldn't get out as the state trooper's and Kyle's cruisers were blocking the exit. He thumbed out the window. "Move your vehicles. NOW!"

Trooper Callaway made a beeline for his cruiser but not Kyle. Oh no, Kyle had to be a thorn in his side. Kyle leaned against his open window, pressing him for an answer.

"I'm not moving it until you tell me where you're going."

"Yeah, where are you heading?" Hugh asked, sidling up beside him. "We've got work here."

"Sorry, Hugh. I've got to go. You'll need to handle Nate from here."

He raised a hand. “Whoa, whoa, Travis, hold up. But what about this?” he said pointing to the birds.

He shrugged. “Right now, Emily and Anna need me.” Travis stuck the gear into reverse and eyed his side mirror, waiting for Callaway to move his vehicle over to one side.

“You want to move yours too?” he asked Kyle.

Kyle tapped the door. “Sure. Where are they?”

“Kyle, I don’t have time for this shit.”

“I have a right to know.”

“Albany. Okay. Someone’s taken, Anna.”

“What?!” he bellowed. “Who?”

This was news to him. He’d told him about the accident as that was all he knew until Emily told him. “That’s what we’re trying to establish. Now if you’d just get out of the way, I need to leave.”

“Are you taking Lucas with you?”

“No, I’m dropping him off at my sister’s.” He held the phone against his chest, waiting for a call. Emily had told him she would phone back in a minute once she had more information. He was curious to know how she knew where Anna was heading.

“Well then, I’m coming with you,” Kyle said, turning to leave.

“Uh, no.”

“Uh, yeah, she’s my daughter, Travis.”

His words hung in the air. He couldn’t argue with that. No matter what the court or lawyers had said, Kyle wasn’t going to take no for an answer and there was no way Emily would speak to him. If he didn’t agree, Travis knew he’d just be an ass and leave his cruiser in the way. “All right. But move your vehicle as we are burning daylight.” Kyle double-timed it to his cruiser and hopped in. He reversed out, almost backing into a tree.

"Again, sorry to leave you, Hugh, but..."

"I'll let dispatch know. If I can get through to them," he muttered.

Travis nodded as he reversed, spun out the truck, and floored it. The tires chewed up dirt as he accelerated, reaching speeds of up to ninety down some of the narrow roads on the way back to town.

Thoughts raced as his truck barreled over dead birds littering the road.

What the hell had caused this?

It would take a good thirty minutes before he would reach the Wilson House Inn, lodgings that had once belonged to the family of Steph's deceased husband, Paul. Steph had lost him to an aneurysm three years after getting married. It almost broke her. That was six years ago. She'd remained single since.

Travis veered around Kyle's cruiser.

"You okay, Lucas?"

He wasn't but he was putting on a brave face.

"Who's taken, Anna?"

"I don't know."

He wanted answers. They all did. But it was as much a mystery as the event they were in. He was only glad they didn't live in a large city. He couldn't imagine the pandemonium they were experiencing or what might unfold because of this. People were creatures of habit. Many criminals were opportunistic. It wouldn't take much to tip the scales toward anarchy.

The road curved around as they got closer to town.

The rural community of Eden Falls was a part of

Bennington County and had just under three thousand residents, a far cry from the thirty-seven thousand spread over numerous towns with Bennington being the largest.

Travis and his sister Stephanie were born and raised in the foothills of Glastonbury Mountain and the shadow of the Green Mountain National Forest. His father had died in his early fifties of liver disease from drinking too much alcohol, and their mother was in a nursing home in Bennington.

The phone rang as he white-knuckled it all the way. Travis tapped the button on the steering wheel to accept the call.

"I can see her," Emily said.

"What?"

"Anna. In the app."

His brow furrowed. "I'm lost. You're going to need to give me a little more than that." He overtook traffic and multiple accidents, picking up speed. He narrowly missed another car as he blew through an amber light just as it was turning.

"Apple has a way to track the location of all devices through an app, Share My Apple ID and Share Location."

"So, tracking her device. Okay, but you have her phone, don't you?"

"I know. But she has an Apple Watch. Inside the Find My app, the watch is listed under her devices."

"But I thought that relied on having the phone with the watch."

"For the GPS version, not the cellular one. I got her the cellular one. It can function independent of the phone. I got her a plan. I wanted to make sure I had a way to contact her just in case she lost her cell phone."

"So, we can phone her?"

"You can, I can't because it uses the same number."

"But what about text?"

"Yeah, I can send one to myself and it will show up on the watch. I've also gone into the watch app, the settings, and sounds and haptics, and set it to silent mode so she should get only the haptic alert, not a sound. I think that's how it works."

"Hold on, Emily. You think? Listen to me, if you send her a message and the volume is not down, they could hear it. It might be best not to text. Just use the tracking."

Emily continued. "Anyway, I can see her moving. She's going north out of the city. Where are you right now?" Emily asked.

"About to drop Lucas off at my sister's. It's on the way. Hey look, Kyle knows. He's following."

"You told him?"

He could hear the tone of her voice drop.

"I had no choice; he came out to an incident."

He heard Emily let out a painful cry.

"Emily. Emily! What's going on?"

"It's my leg. It hurts so bad. Listen, Travis, I have around 50 percent battery life left in this phone, it should last a while. Just hurry up. Anna doesn't have her insulin. If we don't find her soon, she..." she trailed off choking up.

"I hear you, hon, I'll let you know when I'm heading out."

She collected herself and continued. "I'll call you in five minutes. I'll need to shut down to save power."

She disconnected.

Travis shot Lucas a look.

"It's all right, kid. We'll find her."

He hoped he could deliver on that promise.

Travis veered off the main stretch through a gated area up a long driveway that circled a fountain outside a two-story, yellow clapboard farmhouse with a white wraparound porch and black shutters. In the height of summer, the English-style grounds with perfectly trimmed hedges looked every bit as inviting as the home. "Why can't I come with you?" Lucas asked.

"Because you'll be safer here."

"But I want to help."

"And you will, but right now, kid, I need you to stay put until I get back."

"Is my sister going to die?"

He wanted to lie to him, put his mind at ease, but Lucas was a smart kid, both of them were. As much as he wanted to say they got that from their mother, Kyle wasn't a stupid man, he'd just made several stupid decisions. "You have my word. I will do everything I can to bring her back safely."

"And my mother?"

"Her too."

It was promising a lot especially since they were relying on dubious technology and he had no idea what the situation was like out there or what it would become. Lucas turned in his seat and looked out through the rear window of the truck. "Is he going with you?"

"It seems so."

Although Kyle said he'd never lashed out at his kids, and Emily hadn't mentioned it, there was still a sense that Lucas was afraid of his father. Did he know more than his mother? He eased off the gas and pulled up outside, then got out.

Steph pushed open the storm door and stepped out.

She was a beautiful woman. Green eyes, long blonde hair that was tied back in a loose ponytail. That day she had on a jean shirt, black slacks, and white flats. In her mid-forties, she still had a youthful appearance that had attracted numerous men since her husband's death but she'd yet to go out on another date. It was her strength that Travis admired. Her willingness to pick herself up and carry on when others might have crumbled from grief. He honestly wasn't sure how she managed some days with all that needed to be done around the property. She said the work kept her sane.

Sill, despite the loss, she'd grown the business to great heights, so much that it had won awards and been listed as one of New England's finest inns.

"Travis, I was about to call, do you know..." she trailed off, no doubt about to probe for answers to the mysterious event when she laid eyes on the county cruiser pulling up behind his truck.

He glanced over his shoulder as the cruiser slowed to a crawl. "Look, I need you to take Lucas for a while."

"Why? Where's Emily?"

"There's been an accident and..." He glanced down at Lucas. "Look, I don't have time to explain. Can you take him?"

"Of course," she said, extending a hand. Lucas moved to her side and she wrapped an arm around his shoulders. "Travis, what's going on? All these birds and—"

He ignored the questions; it wasn't because he didn't have answers, he could take a stab, a rough guess, but it wouldn't change the situation and right now he had more pressing matters to deal with. "I don't have any clothes for him but..."

Kyle got out of his cruiser, rested his arm on top of the door, and removed his mirrored shades. "Steph."

"Kyle," she replied.

They exchanged a cold glance. Travis had already filled her in on the accusations made by Emily. Steph didn't have any room for men lifting a hand to a woman. It wasn't a sign of strength but weakness. "Travis, have you seen the news?"

"Some of it," he said, reaching into the truck and grabbing out his phone.

"So, you've seen the fish?"

"What?" he responded, puzzled.

"You should come in and see this."

"I don't have time. Emily will be calling me soon. I need to be on the road." He motioned with his arm in a random direction. "I'm an hour away from her and probably even more from Anna."

The words came out fast, not thinking.

"Anna? Isn't she with her?"

He let out a lungful of air. "Someone's taken her."

"What?"

"As I said, there's no time to explain."

"Before you leave, you need to come in and see this. Both of you."

Inviting Kyle into her home? There was no way that would happen under normal circumstances.

Kyle gave a nod and made his way up the porch, following the two of them inside. She led them into the living room, a gorgeous space that reminded him of a Cape Cod-style abode with light blue, white, and yellow décor. There was a large flatscreen TV above a stone fireplace. It was tuned into a news channel where a helicopter was flying over the East Coast, capturing images of fish floating on the ocean. There were thousands. "What the hell?" Kyle said, leaning in and squinting.

"And that's not all," she said, taking the remote and changing to another channel which streamed back even more shocking images of fish in lakes, rivers, and streams. Steph surfed through the channels, one after another. If the media weren't reporting on birds, the focus was on fish, and just like the birds, it was occurring across the country. Millions were dead, washing up on the shores, others blotting out the surface of the water, nothing more than waves of fish.

"Turn it up," Travis said.

Steph increased the volume.

"As you can see, thousands of dead fish have surfaced off the East Coast. Officials are unsure right now and experts are scrambling for answers. In what started with birds falling from the sky and had biologists thinking it was some new kind of bird flu or man-made environmental mess, others are now dismissing this and are suggesting that it could be a terrorist attack. However, our media sources report this is occurring elsewhere, leading many to believe it's some kind of apocalyptic event. The birds began falling under an hour ago. We are waiting to hear if this... hold on... we are learning that what was believed to be only here in America is occurring in nations around the world." The news began broadcasting footage from different countries.

Travis swallowed hard. His throat went dry as he tried to comprehend what he was seeing. India. Russia. China. Africa. South America. France. Germany. The UK. The images flooded in one after the other, an endless stream of inexplicable death. Some of the footage was amateur, recorded on cell phones and uploaded to video sites, showing birds falling into a city of traffic, or fishermen out on a lake overwhelmed as their boats were surrounded and filled by mounds of fish and birds.

In his line of work, Travis had come across all forms of animal ailments, most of it though was isolated to cattle or a few species in a community, and when testing was completed, it was usually pinned down to some disease. The only other time he'd seen such a mystery was when more than three hundred and fifty elephants were found walking in circles only to drop dead. Scientists said something had been attacking their neurological system and later it was proved to be Cyanobacteria, a toxic bacterium that occurred naturally in standing water, growing into large blooms referred to as blue-green algae. But again, it was an event that was isolated to one region, one species, one nation, not this wide and not this sudden.

He chewed over the thought of birds falling into the ocean, spreading something. Had it begun in them first?

If it was some disease that could cross from one species to another, it had to be manmade as it was moving too fast.

As they continued watching more reports, his phone rang reminding him to get moving.

6

New York

Anna returned to awareness drifting in some dreamlike state.

Her skull felt like it was in a vise being crushed on both sides, a headache hammering at the back of her eyes.

Her vision.

It was dark, the world had become muted.

A piece of soft material was wrapped around her face and over her ears.

Instinctively she tried to bring a hand up to pull it away but she couldn't. Her arms were restrained behind her back, something biting at her wrists. Groaning, and moving ever so slightly, she felt a hand press against her as she tried to move.

"She's waking up."

"Give her some more."

She could just make out the shapes of something beyond the cloth.

Voices. A gruff male, someone slightly younger, a woman.

"This wasn't the plan."

"Plans change."

The memory returned fast and furious; birds falling, the accident, her mother trapped, the phone call to Travis, attempting to get help, a black truck stopping, and a woman approaching her, followed by...

Abduction.

It played fast in her mind.

There was little she could do. Her eyes had gone wide, her mouth agape. A large smelly cloth went over her face and words failed to escape her lips. She'd tried to fight, digging her elbows into the brute holding her from behind, but at twelve there was little she could do against a man of his size. The more she struggled, the weaker she became. Darkness crept in at the corner of her eyes as she succumbed to the strange smell that she'd sucked into her lungs.

She swore she heard her mother's voice screaming her name. But the noise of the world around her melted behind the damp cloth.

Tears rushed to the brim of her eyes. Fear taking hold. Her heartbeat sped up. She didn't need anyone to explain the danger to her. It was evident. Anna had heard of girls being taken but that occurred when no one was watching, at night, while walking alone, not on a highway in full view of people.

It dawned on her. No one was watching. No one was paying attention.

The chaos of the moment took precedence — the pain, anguish, fear, fire, and smoke were the focus, not her. Not a small kid whose cry didn't get beyond her lips.

And now here she was, hands tied, eyes covered, and she was moving in a vehicle but to where? And with who?

"Where am I?"

No reply, just the steady hum of the engine.

"Who are you?"

Again nothing.

"Please. Just let me go."

"Keep quiet," the woman said.

"I want my mom," she said, trying to sit up.

"I said, keep quiet." A hand slapped her across the face, knocking her back down.

"Give her some more," the man added.

"Where's my mom?"

"Hurry up," the gruff voice said. "And hold her legs." The truck bounced and veered off. If she'd only been awake the entire time, she might have been able to remember which way they'd gone, counted how many turns or times they stopped. She could have listened for sounds and plotted out some kind of escape where she could retrace her steps. But they'd been clever.

Anna felt bile in her throat. "I'm going to be sick. Stop, let me out."

"Get it on her."

"I'm trying but you need to slow down."

"God, do I have to do everything myself?"

She heard the truck slow. It had worked. The moment they removed the blindfold and untied her hands she'd make a run for it. The tires left a smooth road and went over gravel. She felt the truck swerve, then the brakes take hold. The front door clattered open and then she felt a gust of wind as the door nearest to her head opened.

A hand held her head down and she knew she wasn't being let out.

Anna began kicking like a wild horse. "You little bitch!" the woman said.

"I told you to hold her."

"This better be worth it."

"Just get it on her now."

Anna heard a splash, like the sound of liquid moving in a bottle, and then a damp cloth touched her face, the same one as before. She recognized that pungent smell. It was the same one they'd pushed in her face. Chloroform.

She tried to twist away but the hand was too strong.

"Hold still."

She let out a yelp as someone punched her in the stomach. The rough hands clamped over her mouth smelled like cigarettes and shit, and then it all vanished as her eyes became heavy and each kick of her legs got weaker until they were nothing more than small spasms.

OVER FORTY-FIVE MILES north of Albany just outside Gansevoort, the GMC rolled up alongside a cream-and-white 2003 Winnebago. The home on wheels had been bought with cash from an ad years earlier. They'd dumped a considerable amount of money into it to get it up to living standards. There was to be no record of them and no central place from which they would operate. It was easier that way. People got caught staying in one place, holding down a residence. It made people ask too many questions which led to mistakes and time in the pen. Bill Drayton had no intention of going back to jail. There was too much at stake, big money on the table, far more than he'd been guaranteed and he had every intention of collecting.

In the RV park, the vehicle blended in. People came and went. It wasn't like neighbors would be familiar with their comings. He parked a few feet away from the Class A diesel pusher. Behind the darkly tinted windows, he looked around, surveying his field of vision. They'd selected a lot in the far back, close to the forest, away from prying eyes. Just because they were travelers, out-of-state visitors, that didn't mean folks weren't nosy. Marcus was waiting for them outside, sitting in a folding armchair, a beer cracked open and listening to a radio with a set of headphones on. Beside it, a scanner would keep them one step ahead of the law.

At this stage he couldn't imagine the law being a problem, not after the weird event that had transpired. Whatever it was, it had done him a favor. It was a spur-of-the-moment decision, a flash of creativity that dropped into his head from what Pam would have called an epiphany from the almighty.

Birds falling from the sky? What next? Frogs? Pam had been harping on at him ever since they'd left the highway that it was some religious event, a sign of the end times, but he didn't buy it. He didn't believe in Santa Claus, or any deity, only what he could see with his own two eyes. And he planned to feast them on lots of green before this was over.

Marcus rose, cigarette in his mouth. He flipped up the shades on his prescription glasses. He ran both hands through greasy curly hair, grinning like a fool.

He was wearing a white tank top, baggy cargo pants, and sneakers. For a man of thirty-six, he still dressed like a teenager. Younger brother to Pam, everywhere she went he wasn't that far behind. Like a lost puppy dog. She said she owed him, that their upbringing hadn't been good and now she was making amends or some shit like that. Bill found him to be a pain, an annoying third wheel who tended to interrupt him, especially when he was having sex with his Pam. Still, he'd become quite an asset to him over the years. The way he saw it, he needed foot soldiers, guys willing to do the dirty jobs without knowing a lot of details, and four eyes fit the bill perfectly.

Having two siblings at his beck and call gave him a way to play them off each other.

Twisting toward the BBQ, Marcus lifted the top, letting a plume of smoke rise around him as he took tongs and turned hotdogs. As Bill got out, Marcus hollered over his shoulder. "Right on time."

"Always," Bill replied. "Get her out."

"Get who out?"

Bill held the rear door of the cab open and Marcus turned to see Pam reaching in and lifting the young girl. "Well don't stand there. Give her a hand," Bill said, walking past Marcus and going inside the RV to get himself a beer. The whole thing had gone better than he planned. He had this odd event to thank for that. Unscrewing the cap off a cold bottle, he downed half of it in one gulp and then pressed it against the side of his neck as Marcus and Pam entered carrying sleeping beauty.

"Bill, who is this? This wasn't the plan."

"It is now. Put her in the back and make sure she's tied down. I don't want any mistakes. I'm getting my money's worth out of that one."

The steps outside the RV groaned beneath him as he exited and took a seat where Marcus had sat. He looked up into the bright sky, took a pack of Camels off a small folding table, and tapped one out. Perching it between his lips, he lit it and then picked up his phone to make the call.

Marcus came out, all spit and fury.

"We had an agreement. You want to break that?"

"I don't break it. I make it. I'm the one that sets the rules and if you want a cut, you'll zip it and let me make a phone call to my cousin." He tapped the contact and waited. A moment later, Jackson "Rooster" Shepard answered.

"Rooster. What's the news?"

"The eagle has landed. I've got him in my sights."

"Good. Now don't screw this up. We've got far too much riding on this. Remember what I said, I'll call you every hour. You know what to do if I don't."

He hung up.

"I don't like this. Did you know?" Marcus asked his sister.

Pam shrugged, placing a hand around Bill's shoulders. She knew her place, where her bread was buttered and what would happen if she spoke out of turn.

"Settle down and serve me up one of those hotdogs. It's going to be fine. Just fine." Bill looked across the RV lot at the multiple downed birds. It was a mess and one that would soon stink to high heaven. Who was going to clean this up?

He had thought the incident on Highway 90 was a one-off, a fluke, an act of God. But the feathered bastards were everywhere, all up the main stretch. They'd had to go off the main arteries because the traffic was clogged.

He took one of the earbuds and stuck it in his ear and listened to the scanner.

It was pure pandemonium. The cops didn't know their ass from their heads. Call after call, their hands were tied with accident scenes galore. It would take days, maybe even weeks to clear the roads, never mind get EMTs to the injured.

The timing couldn't be any more perfect.

Now that he had the upper hand, he planned to capitalize on it. For so many years he'd been playing second fiddle to the man, bending over backward, turning the cheek when he wanted to lash out, and now it was all about to change.

But first, he would chill, have a beer, and see what the shill slingers in the news were saying about this event. BBQ smoke wafted in his direction, making his stomach grumble. He took another swig of his drink and then changed the radio station to a major news channel.

As Marcus flipped burgers and rolled hotdogs with the tongs, he glanced his way. "I don't get it. I thought this would be over once you got back. You're only going to bring the cops down on us."

"Do you see any cops?" Bill said.

"I've seen a few roll in here."

"Yeah, well now they have their hands full and we'll be on the move soon."

He took another swig. Bill turned up the volume on the radio.

"What is happening? That's what people are demanding to know. It's been several hours since the birds fell, and large numbers of fish were found floating in lakes, rivers, and oceans. So far there have been no further reports of any other animal deaths but questions are still arising. What we do know is that top military officials are preparing to roll out the National Guard in response to what could become a breakdown of society as people of all nations react to this. How will this affect the economy? Will this endanger the waterways? And what are the long-term effects? It's unknown right now. But first and foremost, scientists are scrambling to figure out if this is some kind of airborne pathogen that could affect humans. So far there are no signs of that. Thank God. Tune in later

to find out as we bring in a panel of experts to discuss the impact this will have on the biosphere, the oxygen levels, and the livelihoods of millions working within the global commercial fishing industry, which we know accounts for hundreds of billions of dollars every year, and countless jobs including the tourism industry."

Marcus switched it off, causing Bill to look up at him.

"You want to explain?" Marcus asked.

"Not right now. I want to relax."

He switched the radio back on only to have Marcus turn it off again. Bill tore out the earbud from his right ear and got up from his seat. "Do we have a problem?"

"We do when you make snap decisions without involving us."

"You're here. You're involved. Satisfied?"

"That's not what I mean. Why did you take her?"

Bill scoffed, placing an arm around Marcus' shoulder. "Marcus. How about you leave the thinking to me and you stick to serving up hotdogs."

"Oh, screw the hotdogs."

"No, they're burning."

He twisted to see. "Damn it!"

Bill snorted. A heavy waft of charred meat hit them and Marcus rushed over and lifted the lid. A blast of hot smoke barreled around him. Bill shook his head and took a seat. "There's your answer. I make the decisions because you can't see the bigger picture. You want answers now. Patience, my friend. All will be revealed. If I left this in your hands we'd be jailed and tossed in the electric chair to fry like those hotdogs." He chuckled as he slipped the earbud back in his ear and tuned back into the news while Marcus muttered to himself.

It was all a matter of timing. Just as it had been to grab her. They would make this work. Plans were adaptable. People predictable. There were times like this that he couldn't help but wonder if Pam was right. Perhaps there was a deity moving the chess pieces behind the scenes, making all things work for the good of his creation, and this was just another one of those moments. A shift on the board, a potential challenge to mankind. What would their next move be? For him, he knew, and it didn't end in a stalemate. It ended with the extinction of everything that a man loved. An end to the games where the spoils were his and there was only one victor, him.

Bill slapped Pam on the ass cheek. "Go grab me another beer."

7

Vermont

"They've stopped moving," Emily said as Travis exited his sister's home. If ransom was the motive, neither one of them had heard from the kidnappers, then again it was still too early to say, as there were several reasons why someone might take a kid and ransom was only one.

Travis didn't want to even imagine what they might be doing to Anna.

He knew the stats, the outcome of most abductions. Twenty-four hours was being generous. His eyes scanned the ground, looking at the dead birds, trying to make sense of it. If he wasn't dealing with this right now, he would have been knee-deep in collecting birds and fish and sending them off for testing.

"Listen, Emily. I know you don't want to think about this but, they may have found the watch and tossed it away."

"For Anna's sake, I hope not," Emily shot back.

Travis caught the fear in her tone, her voice cracking ever so slightly. He couldn't begin to imagine the strain she was feeling. Not only had she been in a car accident but she'd had to witness her daughter being taken and was unable to help.

On any other day an Amber Alert would have gone out, state patrol would have been on the lookout for that truck. But not now. There were too many in need of help.

He couldn't wrap his head around it.

Sure, a strange event wouldn't stop people from doing whatever they'd set out to do that day, whether good or bad, but this was brazen. It seemed so odd for a couple to just snatch a kid up in the middle of a highway, in broad daylight. Even those lacking a few brain cells were careful. It wasn't like the electrical grid was down. Some of the highways and bridges now had CCTV that monitored traffic and accidents. Even if it never picked up the two engaged in the act of scooping Anna up, it would likely have the vehicle on camera, especially since Emily had the license plate. It was a New York plate. "Travis, I need you to go to my house. In the fridge is another travel case of insulin. You're going to need to take that with you."

"Look, with Kyle coming, maybe he can head over to you?"

"No. You don't get it. There's no time. She's going to need that insulin soon."

"I know, I meant in a different vehicle."

"Travis, there's no telling when these people are going to be on the move again and who knows how many there are. You'll need his help."

"What if I can get someone else to come to you?"

"No. After. I can survive here for now. Get to my girl."

The mother in her was coming out, hard and fast. She cared very little for herself. Her kids were her life, and a large reason why she left Kyle in the first place. She didn't want to raise them in an environment that was toxic. Though according to her, it wasn't always that way. He'd been a good father, that was the one thing she'd said positively about Kyle. He would walk over hot coals for his kids.

It was a pity he wouldn't do the same for his wife.

The panic and fear of the unknown were before them. Based on the information Emily had given, she was a good hour away but with the accidents on the roads and clogged highways, that might as well have been triple. Anna, meanwhile, was around forty miles from them. It was pretty much the same but the difference was, Anna couldn't afford to go without insulin. Time was ticking. Without it, her sugar levels would spike, which could be exacerbated by stress and dehydration. All of which could result in life-threatening ketoacidosis in less than a day.

As a multi-daily injection user, taking one long-acting insulin in the evening and rapid insulin before each meal, Anna could start feeling uncomfortable within twelve hours of missing a dose. The short-acting ones took effect within ten to fifteen minutes but they only lasted around four and a half hours. No two diabetics were the same. Body types, age, the kind of diabetes they had, and how their body responded to medication all were a factor in how they could react. Travis couldn't help but feel sorry for the kid. She'd barely started her life and she was already dealing with an uphill battle. Emily had given him the rundown on it when he first met Anna. She referred to her life with diabetes as like walking a tightrope, where she was forever teetering between highs and lows and the possibility of seizure, coma, and death.

"I'll do my best."

The thought of failing her was only exacerbated by the past.

"I think we should ride together," Kyle said as Travis was getting in. "I can't take the cruiser."

"Have you squared it away with the department? Leaving, I mean."

"Have you?" Kyle scoffed.

He was half listening as he fired up the engine. "Whatever, man, get in."

The fact was neither of them could get in contact with dispatch. They were inundated with calls, or the system had gone kaput due to the event. But at least he'd told Hugh.

Kyle locked his cruiser by hitting the key fob. It let out a beep, the lights flashed, then he came around the back of the truck and hopped in. Steph and Lucas stared out of the window as they peeled out, leaving a plume of grit and dirt in their wake. The truck rumbled over uneven ground as he fishtailed out of the driveway and increased speed. Having him in his truck felt uncomfortable. They'd already exchanged more words in the past half an hour than they had in the entirety of knowing one another. Kyle's eyes roamed the cab, looking in the back at his gear. He even popped the glove compartment to peek at what was inside.

"You mind?" Travis said.

Kyle closed it with a wry grin. "Clean. Orderly. This whole event must be throwing you for a real loop. So, what did my wife have to say?" he asked, emphasizing the phrase "my wife." He still hadn't gotten it through his head that it was truly over.

"We've got to pick up the insulin pack from the house."

"Did she forget it?"

"No, Kyle, she didn't," he said, making it clear before he started speaking badly about her. A common trait among those who had split.

Kyle sniffed hard. "You know, if you swing by my place, I could grab my car and you could head to Anna while I collect her."

"That's not what she wants."

"Of course it isn't. What Emily wants is what Emily gets." Another jab. It was to be expected. It wasn't anything out of the norm from the months gone by when he'd shown up at a restaurant while the two of them were out together. That had been awkward. "By the way, how does she know where Anna is?"

"Apple. Tracking," Travis said while gripping the wheel tighter. He had a sense that as short or long as the journey might be, he was going to regret agreeing to let him ride along.

Kyle brought his head back with his mouth wide. "Gotta love technology. I don't recall my daughter having a phone but then again, there are a lot of things Emily's allowed since my leaving."

"Look, Kyle, I understand you're here because of your daughter. But because we're going to be together for a while, whatever problems you have with Emily, while you're riding with me, I'd appreciate it if you kept them to yourself. We'll get along much better that way."

Kyle snorted and gave a half-assed salute. "You got it, captain."

Emily's home was in the southern region of Eden Falls just off Meadowbrook Drive, a quiet new development nestled among the pines. The two-story, three-bedroom saltbox colonial was near the end of a cul-de-sac with just under one acre of property. Among its neighbors, it stood out with clapboard siding, a bright red door, and nine windows with shutters just at the front of the house.

"Well, this brings memories back. You know, I'm surprised you haven't moved in with her yet or the other way around. Have you had that conversation?"

Travis glanced at him. Was he trying to get a rise out of him?

Kyle continued. "I doubt she'll want to give this up. Do you know she had me take her around to fourteen homes before we settled on this one? Back and forth we went, and, once we put in an offer and the paperwork was going through, she changed her mind again. Did she tell you that?" Kyle said smiling as they pulled into the long driveway that came up the right side of the house and stopped in front of a two-car garage. Travis didn't answer. He was baiting him, fishing for details, and he wasn't falling for that. "Yeah, I tried to reason with her but she wouldn't have it. Forced me to contact the real estate agent. Of course, we couldn't do it without breaking the contract. Made me look like a fool."

Yeah, like that would be hard, Travis thought as he killed the engine and got out. Kyle gazed up at the garage. "In the weeks before I moved out, I was sleeping above that garage, on a dingy mattress." He smacked his lips. "Ah, good times," he said, slamming the door shut and making his way around.

Travis gazed at the sprawling green lawn. When he took out the key to the house and unlocked the front door, Kyle chuckled. "You must be doing well. I see she's given you keys to the kingdom. Impressive. So did she give you that on the first date or only after she had sex with you?"

Travis wheeled around, hands balled. He stopped just short of lashing out at him. That would have only given Kyle that much more pleasure, or a reason to fight, and right now that would only slow things down. "Why don't you wait in the truck?"

"Ah, if it's all the same with you, I'd like to take a walk down memory lane," he said, brushing past him and entering the house. He stopped in the doorway and lifted his nose and breathed in. "Oh, the sweet smell of home."

Travis entered behind him and closed the door and made a beeline for the fridge. He opened it and fished around for the insulin case. When he found it, he placed it on the granite-topped kitchen island and unzipped it, and checked. There were several vials of fast-acting insulin inside and orange-capped syringes.

"Don't move!" a female voice bellowed. Travis turned ever so slightly and moved around the corner to see Carla, Emily's sister, pointing a Glock at Kyle's back. Carla was a few years younger than Emily, a petite gal but with a larger-than-life persona that caught anyone who didn't know her off guard. She had short, black hair styled in a way that reminded him almost of Joan Jett. She had a gravelly voice to match. He'd rarely seen her wear much else besides black T-shirts, dark jeans or leopard print pants, and Doc Martens. That day was no different, she wore a Rolling Stones black T-shirt with a big pair of red lips and a tongue sticking out, and ripped blue jeans.

She had a round face and perfectly shaped full lips. A carousel of ink covered her hands and arms in a distracting way. Beautiful in her own way, she had every bit what it might have taken to be a model, but her addiction to drugs had taken her down a slippery path into rehab multiple times. After Kyle had moved out, Carla had moved in. Emily was trying to do her a favor. Give her a place to get back on her feet but as of late, she had started to think her sister was stealing from her to get that next hit.

"One hell of a way to greet family," Kyle said.

"You're not family. What are you doing in here, and how did you get in?"

"Carla, hey, it's okay, I let him in," Travis said, putting out a hand and motioning to her.

"Travis?"

As soon as she saw him, she lowered the gun. "Emily gave me a key," he said. "I'm picking up Anna's insulin." He held it up so she could see.

A frown formed. "But she took it with her this morning."

"I know, didn't she call you?"

She offered back a confused expression. "No. What's happened?"

Kyle chuckled, shaking his head. "Figured. Maybe if you dialed back on those opioids, you'd see the world in full color instead of spinning above you," he said, making his way around the kitchen island and fingering a pile of mail on the counter.

Carla stomped across the kitchen and snatched the mail away from him before he could get a chance to go rooting through it. "This isn't your home anymore."

"And I believe it's soon to be not yours either." He smiled. "Yeah, word gets around. Big sis is kicking you out." He sucked air between his teeth. "That's gotta hurt."

Carla glared as she snatched up a pack of Marlboro Lights, tapped one out, and stuck it between her teeth before lighting it with the click of a Zippo. She blew it in Kyle's direction, knowing it would piss him off. He hated it, at least according to Emily, who had once been a long-time smoker. "So?" Carla asked.

"There's been an accident," Travis replied.

"And?"

There wasn't a hint of concern in her reply which caught Travis off guard. He assumed it was because she was annoyed with Emily after she decided to send her packing. Carla had until the end of the week to be out but still, sisters were sisters.

"Someone's taken, Anna."

"Who?"

"That's what we're off to find out," he said, making his way around her, eager to get moving. An invisible countdown was ticking in the back of his mind, aware that the longer they took, the higher the chance that Anna would die — with or without insulin.

"Then I'm going with you."

"I think not," Kyle said with a half chuckle.

"You don't have a say in it."

"That's where you're wrong. Tell her, Travis."

"If she wants to come, that's up to her. She has every right. The more the better," he said. Carla raised her eyebrows and pursed her lips into a smile at Kyle before going to collect a jacket. Travis didn't linger. As he stepped outside and made his way back to the truck, Kyle caught up with him.

"This is a big mistake. The last thing we need is an addict tagging along."

"It's her sister and niece," Travis said without stopping. He set the diabetes cold pack inside the vehicle and glanced out through his rear window at the sound of a throaty muffler. A black Ducati Scrambler 1100 Sport Pro motorcycle came roaring up the driveway. The rider was decked out in black leather gear, his face obscured behind a shiny black visor, but he didn't need to wait until he got off to know who it was.

Danny.

His brother.

It had been a long while since the two of them had talked. Two years of radio silence to be exact. Travis couldn't think of a worse time to see him. Although the situation didn't mirror the past, the stakes were pretty much the same. Two people's lives are on the line, a mother and a child.

"Now who the hell is this?" Kyle muttered, his eyes drifting from Danny to Carla as she locked the door and strolled across to the truck with a backpack slung over her shoulder. Travis made his way over to his brother as he turned off the bike, and removed his helmet with both hands. He had swept-back dark hair that came down to his chin and a patchy beard. He ran a hand through the oily mess and narrowed his gaze.

"This is not the time," Travis said.

"Don't worry, I'm not here for you. Steph filled me in. I want to help."

"I don't have much room in the truck with gear, and taking these two."

Danny looked over to them.

"Doesn't matter. I'll follow. I'll stay out of your way... besides," he muttered, pointing to the dead birds on the lawn and driveway, "seems we might have more than kidnappers to contend with. You can rely on me."

That last part was a jab. A comment he'd used before, on that fateful day.

While Travis wanted to dismiss him, send him on his way, it was only because of the way their last conversation had ended did he consider saying yes. The loss in his life had almost destroyed Danny. Having Travis at the heart of it, well, that was the icing on the cake. He blamed him. It was surprising he hadn't gone down the same route as Carla except drugs weren't his vice, hard liquor was, and lots of it. Anything to numb the emptiness.

"Sure. Why not."

"I'll tell you why not!" Kyle said.

"Oh, put a sock in it," Travis said, taking his phone and calling Emily for directions. Right now, she would be their eyes, like a GPS voice guiding them.

"What's the update?" he asked.

"No movement, yet."

"How far out?"

"An hour but..."

"Yeah, we'll add another two or three hours to that."

"Exactly," she replied.

A pause.

"Look, your sister is coming with us, my brother too. Are you sure you don't want me to have them come to you?"

"It would only be a waste of time; besides, I have no idea if they'd make it here. Things are heating up, Travis. The traffic jam hasn't improved. A lack of EMTs has people losing their minds. Tempers are boiling over." She paused to reel in her emotion. "Travis, if she's..."

"She's not."

"But if she dies..."

"She won't."

He wanted to assure her but he knew in doing so, the same words might be used against him later, the same way his brother had done with his wife, Shailene. "Has anyone contacted Kyle about a ransom?"

"Not so far."

"God. I can't believe this has happened. Why would they do this?" she asked.

Travis took a deep breath, considering the most obvious reason. Emily wished him well then hung up. He turned toward the others, aware that this was going to be one hell of a journey where no one's life was guaranteed.

8

It was a warning sign of something far worse to come.

The four guests checking out were unable to hide the fear. It was stamped on their faces and revealed in the way they carried themselves and the speed with which they exited. Two of the families hadn't stayed the full number of days and not one of them asked for a refund. They almost looked embarrassed but it was understandable.

Since the inexplicable and sudden death of birds and fish around the globe, fresh news had hit the airwaves of widespread panic buying of food, water, and gasoline. Talk of the president declaring a state of emergency and the deployment of the National Guard was already on experts' lips though they had yet to pull the trigger. What had caused this? Steph sat perched on the edge of the sofa glued to the TV while Lucas chomped on a bowl of noodles, texting his friends, seemingly oblivious to the encircling madness.

She tapped her lower lip and thought about what they had in the way of supplies. While she would fare better than most as unlike a regular family, she was often feeding far more than four or five mouths, a trip to Costco was still tempting.

"Stephanie, do you have any soda pop?"

"Yeah, it's in the pantry, help yourself."

Distracted, she got up and grabbed a pad of paper from a drawer and a pen, and headed into the kitchen to take stock of what she had, what she would need. It dawned on her that barring the essentials, and the two generators that she kept on hand for storms, she hadn't given much thought to what she might need or do if an emergency arose.

The cops, EMTs, a hospital, all of it was one phone call away.

They'd experienced a few power outages but nothing that had gone beyond a few days. Disasters were manageable. Temporal. Hell, it was a common occurrence across the country, so much so that most had become accustomed to and even expected it. But not this. While news channels hadn't thrown out any numbers, they hadn't painted a pretty picture either. The fishing industry was huge, far greater than most imagined. Even if it had only affected a small percentage of aquatic life around the world, it could have catastrophic effects on jobs and the economy. And if it was a total wipeout of all fish, that could send the world into a downward spiral.

She tried to remain composed, wishing Travis or her husband were here. As a single woman, she'd faced pressure from friends and family to meet someone and she'd considered it. But finding the time. Sitting in a bar alone. Wading through a series of bad dates. The very thought of it made her blood pressure skyrocket.

The loss of Paul to an aneurysm had sent her life into a spin. She'd only gotten three years with him. They were good years but not enough. Taking over the inn from his parents, talking about having kids of their own, and frequent vacations and summer BBQs with friends was their life, and all of it was taken in one sudden moment. There was no way to prepare for that kind of loss.

She'd been so angry at God. Why him? There were terrible people in the world that did all manner of horrible things. Paul was good. He was the type of person that would have given you the shirt off his back. The day it happened, he was outside clearing the leaves out of the gutters when she heard the ladder crash. She came racing out and thought he was just unconscious. That he would wake up in the hospital with a few broken bones but that would be the extent of it.

He wouldn't be that lucky.

Steph crossed to where her laptop was on the oak table. She fired it up and did a quick search for an emergency plan. It didn't take long to find one that was meant to help a person last three days. She figured she would just extend the basics of that list and buy extra of everything. Better to have two of something than run out.

"Stephanie, I can't find the pop."

"It's on the bottom shelf. You might have to dig for it."

A few moments later, he yelled, "Found it."

She chuckled. Kids. Unless it jumped out at them, it didn't exist.

As she browsed the website of a national emergency service, she noticed that none of the disasters listed — earthquakes, floods, home fires, heat waves, hurricanes, landslides, power outages, thunderstorms, tornadoes, tsunamis, wildfires, winter storms — were what they were facing. Where was the death of birds and fish?

They were entering new territory.

Still, after a few minutes of browsing, she found a generic emergency list.

Steph scrawled down tips from the guide — buy items with a long shelf life, check the expiration dates, rotate out old for new, buy a few items each week to keep your pantry stocked, go for items that don't need to be refrigerated after they're opened, and eat items in order based on their expiration date so none would go to waste.

Lucas came strolling over and plunked down beside her on a stool. Steph hadn't had a chance to get to know Emily. She'd met her a few times and knew about her ex. It was hard to live in Eden Falls and not know about Kyle. His reputation preceded him. Depending on who she spoke to, they either praised him six ways to Sunday, or they tore a strip off him. Fortunately, she hadn't been on the wrong side of the law to see that other side, but according to Travis, many had.

"What are you doing?" Lucas asked, sipping on orange Fanta. The bottle looked almost too big for his face.

"Making a list. We're going to duck into town and collect some supplies. You up for a ride?"

"Sure."

"Well, go get your shoes on. I shouldn't be much longer."

He padded away, sliding across the hardwood floors in his white socks like Tom Cruise in *Risky Business.* "Okay, what do we need?" she muttered. "Water – roughly one liter per person per day, two if there were pets and enough for three days, another two liters for cleaning. Really?" She tapped the pen against her bottom lip. There was so much that she hadn't even considered. Like most, she just expected things would always be there. Water was one. There was a link to springs in the area just in case the water went down and there was no more in the stores. Of course, it would have to be boiled but it was good to know. Next was non-perishable food and a can opener. "Already have that." She scratched that off the list, then paused for a second and added it back on again knowing that with her luck, it would probably break. Ready-to-eat canned food, protein, granola, fruit bars, dry cereal, trail mix, peanut butter, dried fruit, dried meat, the list went on, and one by one she kept adding things while she went back and forth to the pantry.

"All ready?"

"Nearly, I'll be there in a sec."

"Medication, baby supplies. No baby — no need for supplies. That's good. Eyeglasses, contacts, dentures..." Fortunately, she hadn't reached that golden age yet even though she had noticed a few gray hairs. She jotted down pet food and medication for Archer, her small brown dachshund. The list continued. "Ah now, this I do need. Another crank or battery-operated flashlight, additional batteries, a first-aid kit, extra cash, personal hygiene, and a phone charger. Uh!" She groaned. She felt she was behind the curve. Had she known about this event weeks ago, she could have ordered this but in a small town like hers, there were only so many things she could get, the rest would require a drive into the bigger city. "Screw it." She sent the link to her phone and would browse it while she was out.

As Steph slipped into a long thin cream-colored coat, she took one look outside and noticed it was still raining. "They're calling for another storm," Lucas said, holding up his phone to show her the weather forecast.

"Of course they are," she said, unsurprised. "Because the death of birds and fish isn't enough. Go big or go home, that's how we do it here on planet earth," she said sarcastically. It wasn't a joking matter but at that time she didn't fully grasp the extent of what had happened, or what was about to happen and the impact it would have on the lives of everyone on the planet. "Come on, Lucas," she said, stepping outside but not before grabbing up Archer. She took him everywhere. He was small enough to carry. Since she was a kid she'd wanted a sausage dog, the short-legged, long-bodied hound that had become as much a part of the experience of visiting the inn as the inn itself.

They made a mad dash for a hardtop, forest-green Jeep Wrangler. Within minutes, they were inside, pulling out and heading towards the outskirts of town. Usually, she bought most of her food for the inn in bulk at Costco but that wasn't nearby, that was almost two hours away, but they did have a Walmart supermarket, so that would have to suffice.

Lucas cranked up the heat to take the edge off the cool April weather and turned on the radio trying to find a station to listen to music. He stopped on a news channel that was discussing the event. Steph turned it off.

"Hey, I wanted to listen to that."

"I think we've had enough bad news for one day, kiddo."

He dipped his chin. "Hey," Steph said, getting his attention. "It's going to be all right. I'm sure this is just something that is being blown out of proportion. We'll probably wake up tomorrow and they'll have some good explanation like they always do. Like that lake in India that changed color from green to pink."

"It's not that I'm bothered about."

"Lucas," she said. "Travis and your dad will find her and bring your mom back too."

"I hope so."

It was a lot for a ten-year-old to handle, combined with

the strangeness of the day, and it could bring anyone's mood down.

The Jeep snaked its way through the streets until it arrived under the bright floodlights of the Walmart parking lot. There were a couple of large snowplows that had gone through and scooped up dead birds and piled them on the far side of the lot like a snowbank. No doubt it would begin to stink if they didn't dispose of it soon. As evening fell upon them and the sun had almost vanished, shadows began to form, stretching out from vehicles across the lot. Other residents must have had the same idea as them as the lot was packed the way it was at Christmas. After spending a few minutes circling to find a parking space, they ended up parking a good distance from the doors. "All right. In and out. We'll grab what we need and tonight I'll whip you up whatever you want for dinner."

"Really?"

"Yeah. Why not. Let's go crazy. What do you like?"

"Um. Chili."

"I figured a kid like you would ask for pizza."

"It's Anna's favorite. I like it too."

"Then chili it is." She winked at him and got out, her heart feeling heavy and anxious. She cracked the windows and left Archer in the Jeep. There were many stores she could take him in but Walmart wasn't one. Thankfully, he wasn't like most dogs that would yap at strangers. He knew the routine and curled into a ball on the back seat. They wouldn't be long. They made a beeline for the entrance to get out from the rain, their boots splashing through puddles.

Inside, it was busy and stuffy. No one appeared to be acting like lunatics on Black Friday but there was an urgency to the way people were buying. They didn't dawdle or linger.

Items were scooped into carts and people moved with purpose. Each one eyeing others with a look of knowing, a sense that they wished them well through whatever was happening.

When they made it to the aisle where the water was, the shelf was practically bare. She noticed one couple had seven cases stacked in their cart. They eyed her for a second, then the male took off one of the water cases and put it down. His partner looked to take issue with it but he waved her off and gave a smile. "Stay safe," he said.

"Thanks."

Just as she went to grab it, another guy pushed past her and scooped it up. "Hey. That was ours," she said.

"Now it's mine. Snooze you lose." And he was gone like a flash. Not even the guy who'd put it down saw him take it.

The good and the bad, side by side.

"Geesh. It's a dog-eat-dog world," she said, taking several of the more expensive single bottles of water and filling up the cart. After that they hurried through the rest of the list, getting everything they needed and more before checking out and exiting the store. Outside, the rain had stopped, leaving a slick sheen to the lot. Water splashed up her leg as Steph pushed the cart up to the Jeep. She hit the key fob and opened the back. As she began loading bags into the rear, she said, "Go on, hop in, keep Archer company." Lucas got inside. She was just on the last couple of bags when out the corner of her eye she saw a black blur, that's all it was.

The next moment she was on the ground and someone was grabbing her handbag. It happened at such a speed, she didn't even get a chance to chase after the guy. She looked up to see him racing away, looking back over his shoulder with a grin.

A second later, a tall, broad-shouldered man stepped out from between a truck and van and clotheslined the guy with the edge of his forearm, knocking him to the ground. He tussled with the man, pulling him up to his feet. "Go on, get the hell out of here!" he yelled as the guy scrambled away, like a rat fearful for its life.

Holding her bag, he made his way over. "I believe this is yours."

"Thank you."

"You are more than welcome. Are you okay? No broken bones?"

"I don't think so," she said with a smile. "Nothing like that has happened to me before. This is a fairly decent town."

"I expect with all that's happening, it's drawing out the worst in people."

Lucas had gotten out to help her after hearing the scream but she was already up.

"Yeah, I guess," she said, wiping grime off her jacket. "I haven't seen you around."

He smirked, flashing his pearly whites. "Well, there are a lot of people in this town."

"No, I'm pretty good with faces. You tend to see the same types, year in and year out."

"Ah, a local."

"Born and raised," she replied.

"Well, then you're right. That's because I'm not from here. Philadelphia. Just passing through. Heading to my brother's." He pointed in a random direction. "He lives in Burlington. You know it?"

"Ah, yeah, beautiful place," she said, tossing her bag in the back and closing the door. "Spent many a weekend there. Back when I was married."

"Right." He glanced at Lucas. "Well, I should get going. Are you sure you're okay?"

"Fine."

As he turned to walk away, Steph bit down on her lower lip. "Thank you again. I wish I could repay you but uh..."

He stopped. "Well, there is something you could do."

"Name it."

"Point me in the direction of a good inn?"

She laughed. "You're kidding, right?"

"No, I need a place, just for a night or two."

"Well, the stars must have aligned. I own an inn, and right now we are vacant."

"Huh. Well, uh, this is kind of awkward. I mean, I don't want to make this awkward. If you want to direct me to another, I'd be fine with that."

"Give business away? I just had four guests walk out on me. Two had paid ahead, but the others were thinking of staying for a week if they enjoyed their first night. You're more than welcome."

"Okay then. That sounds like a deal."

"We're making chili tonight."

"I love chili." He thumbed over his shoulder. "Well, I'll follow you, okay?"

"Yeah, we're only a few minutes out of town. By the way, my name is Stephanie. But friends call me Steph."

He extended a hand. "Jackson Shepard. But friends call me Rooster."

9

New York

The anguish was unbearable. Emily was torn on what to do. Lost in thought, she turned the iPhone around in her hand then stopped and stared at the screen.

Although unable to phone her daughter using that phone, as the watch and phone shared the same number, she knew she could use iMessage to send a text to herself and it would mirror on the Apple Watch. Her instincts told her to do it but what if Travis was right, what if it made a dinging sound on the watch and her captors heard it? She'd heard Anna get texts from her friends before and it had always dinged. Not loud but loud enough. But that was from someone else, not from the phone that was linked to the watch.

No. Wait. Right now, we have the advantage.

They knew where she was.

Sitting there she couldn't help but wonder what Anna was thinking. The fear she must have felt being grabbed. If she could communicate with her at least that might put her at ease, especially if she knew that help was on the way. It would lift her spirits.

Again, doubt crept in.

But what if the option she changed in settings for sound didn't work? What if they heard the notification sound?

What if it's too loud?

Her captors would throw the watch away if they hadn't done it already and that would screw everything up. Then Travis would have no way of finding Anna, and what little chance they had of recovering her would be gone. On the other hand, if it worked and no one heard, she could be there for her daughter, she could learn more about the captors, where she was being held, and what they'd done to her. Emily felt sick to her stomach at the thought of it. All manner of true stories in the news of girls being taken came to mind. The sexual assaults. The murders. The statistic of survival was low. Most young kids were dead within twenty-four hours.

Emily sighed and took stock of her situation.

The I-90 traffic hadn't improved nor had her pain.

She still hadn't seen or heard an ambulance since the crash. Now as the sun was all but gone, she could feel the chill of the air nipping at her skin. Light rain continued to fall, making her clothes damp. The temperatures weren't high at noon but without the warmth of the day she'd soon grow cold and with an injured right leg, there was a chance she might succumb to her injuries. Food? Water? She hadn't even considered that. She knew you could go days without both.

All she could think about right then was Anna.

Now and again she would hear gunshots and look.

She didn't know if someone had lost their mind, or whether it was cops or victims trying to defend themselves, but it only made her that much more afraid and keen to find a weapon.

Forcing herself up onto her one good leg, she wobbled forward and slowly made her way over to a Toyota sedan and peered inside, hoping to take shelter for a few hours from the weather that wasn't showing signs of letting up. She tried the door but it was locked. There was no one inside but there was a blanket and what looked like a bottle of pop in the center console. Earlier she'd seen occupants of different vehicles take their belongings and begin hiking, hoping to reach a nearby service station or emergency services. Several had passed her. Besides the two that came to her aid earlier, the rest ignored her — perhaps overwhelmed by their own crisis.

Using her elbow, she tapped the middle of the rear window and then gave it a hard strike. It didn't break. She'd seen countless movies where they made it look easier. Instead, she ended up with a sore elbow. "Sonofabitch!"

She really didn't want to have to break into a car if possible. Who knew if the owners would be back? Still, she needed shelter and fast.

Wobbling on one leg, she used the cars to support her.

Emily tried two more vehicles before she found an open door. "Thank God." She popped the trunk, went to the back, fished around inside, and collected a tire iron. With all the fights she'd seen in the last few hours, she wanted to have something on her to protect herself. Grimacing with pain, Emily slipped into the rear seat and laid down.

Another glance at the phone.

Anna's watch was still showing the same location. Was it an apartment, a home, or had they pulled over into a rest stop? What if they had discovered the Apple Watch and tossed it? She'd be taking a huge risk messaging her but if Anna still had it, there was time, a chance they could gain information about where she was, who she was with, names, signs, anything that could help track them down just in case the power on the watch ran out and she could no longer see her in the Find My app.

It was a risk. She went back and forth over it in her mind. If they had taken her for money, they would eventually hear from them, they would talk about a drop-off, a place to collect her. But if not? The thought of how scared her daughter was finally tipped her over the edge.

Emily tapped out a message to herself.

Anna, it's mom. I'm on your phone.

She didn't want to say that they were on their way just in case the captors had it and were looking. She didn't want them to know they were using the device to track her movement. Not everyone was familiar with how it worked. They might just think the device had texting and phone capabilities and that was it.

Apple showed a delivery message.

She waited, staring at the screen. What if they had her hands tied? There was a way to send a text via voice message using Siri, but if she couldn't view the message? She wouldn't know it was from her.

Emily didn't expect an instant response.

Even if she got the message, it might be a while before she was alone and felt safe enough to respond.

Emily lowered the phone and sat up, grimacing with every shift of her body. Breathing was hard, her ribs were in agony. She set the phone down, and lifted her top, and then used the flashlight on the phone to get a better look. There was a huge area around her ribs that was black and blue. She leaned forward and took a cup out from the center console. It was half-filled with cold coffee. She downed it without hesitation. Anything to avoid the thirst.

Ding.

She looked down and her heart leaped at the sight of a message.

Mom. I'm scared. Where are you?

Was it her? Or her captors playing a sick game to find out more? She avoided saying where she was or that Travis was coming. Instead, she fished for an answer, asking a question that only Anna would know the answer to.

A few seconds later, a reply came back with the correct answer.

She asked two more just to be sure. Both times, Anna answered correctly. There was still a chance they were holding the watch and asking Anna for the answers so she stayed tight-lipped about Travis. As difficult as it was to hold that card back, it was the only way she could be sure. Still, she wanted to give her daughter hope even if it was in the form of a lie.

I'm trying to call the cops.

Trying was the word. She knew. Her captors knew that was impossible. Since the accident, she'd called that number multiple times without success.

Still, just telling her that would give her some peace of

mind that she was doing everything within her power to get help to her. From that moment on, the messages back and forth were rapid. There were short delays in between but for every question she asked, an answer was returned.

Darlin', have they hurt you?

No.

Where do they have you?

In some vehicle. I don't know. It's different than the truck.

They'd switched her over into another vehicle. Probably to avoid getting caught. No doubt they would have dumped the truck especially if it was stolen.

How many are there?

I don't know. I've only heard two males, one female.

Have they told you why they took you?

No.

Are you alone?

Yes.

Listen to me, hon, I want you to cover up that watch. Whatever you do don't let them see it. If they ask, it's just a watch.

Understood.

Now how are you feeling?

If and when her blood sugar began to rise, she would start to feel thirsty, she'd want to urinate more, she would feel fatigued, nausea and possibly even vomit. These were just a few of the warning signs that she was all too familiar with.

I'm okay right now.

I want you to do something. Tell them that you are diabetic and that if you don't get insulin you will go into a diabetic coma and die. Maybe they'll drop you off at a hospital, or take you somewhere they can get you insulin.

I got it.

Even though Travis was on the way, there was no guarantee they would make it in time, let alone make it at all. If the back roads were anything like the highways, it wasn't just dead birds dotted all over the ground they had to contend with, it was traffic, accidents, and more people out on the roads searching for supplies to ride out the event. She hadn't had a moment to even think what could have caused it or search the internet. Every second had been focused on watching that Find My app.

And Anna. If it's safe and you can do it, run. You hear me. Get to a house, a store, anyone who can help.

I have to go, mom, they're coming.

I love you.

As silence fell, Emily began to cry. She thumped the seat hard with her fist, anger getting the better of her. How dare they. Who were they?

ANNA FELT like a penned animal in the bedroom, waiting for them to walk in.

The room, if it could even be called that, as it felt more like a cell, was big enough to fit a queen-size mattress with a narrow gap around the edges so a person could access the shallow dresser and closets. What was this place? Where was she?

Above was a dome light that illuminated the pine 1980s-style cupboards. There were two windows, one on either side, covered by blinds, and a side lamp to her left and right.

Although it was comfortable it was still a prison and they had made sure she knew that by keeping her secure. The only difference now from the first time she'd woken up was they had zip-tied her hands in front of her, which had allowed her to see the text from her mother.

Just being able to chat with her gave her hope.

She'd remembered getting the watch, thinking that her mother was acting like Big Brother when she pointed out that it had a feature that would let her track her location, but now, she was more grateful than ever.

Anna had no idea that she was in an RV until the raggedy-looking woman, the same one from the truck, slid open the accordion pocket door and she got a clear shot of the rest of the motor home. Anna shuffled back on the bed, trying to put some distance between her and her captor.

"Ah, good, you're awake." She entered with a Burger King box, a large Pepsi drink, and fries. There was no introduction, no name given. "Figured you'd be hungry." She set it down on a small side table.

"Why are you doing this?"

"No questions. Just eat."

"I feel sick."

"That's just the chloroform. It'll wear off. Now eat."

"A little hard with these on," she said, lifting her wrists.

"That's why they're in front of you. You can still lift food to your mouth."

"Hardly."

Anna's gaze darted to the doorway at the sound of someone new entering the vehicle. It was another man, younger than the brute that had manhandled her into the truck. He glanced at Anna, snatched up some cigarettes, and exited. She noticed it was dark outside. How long had she been asleep?

"Don't even think about it," the woman said. "There's nowhere to go."

She wanted Anna to believe that she was helpless, at their mercy. In some ways she was. "Here, I'll help." The woman took out the burger dripping with ketchup. She brought it up to Anna's mouth but she turned her face away. The woman scowled.

"Eat," she said, pressing the bread against her lips in a forceful manner.

"No."

"Eat!"

"No!"

Anna kept her lips pursed.

"Suit yourself." The woman dumped it in the box as if it was no skin off her nose. She tried to bring the Pepsi to her mouth, placing the tip of the straw against her lower lip. "C'mon, you've got to be thirsty."

"What is it?"

"Pop."

"If I drink that I'll probably die."

"It's not poison."

"To me, it can be."

"Don't be stupid, all kids love pop."

"Well, I'm not like all kids. I'm diabetic. Without taking insulin before I eat or drink, my blood sugars are going to soar even faster than they are now."

The woman froze, a frown slowly forming. "So, what does that mean?"

It wasn't uncommon to hear that from strangers. Not everyone knew what it meant to be diabetic, the dangers they faced, the restrictions they had.

"It means if I don't get insulin and fast, I'll go into a coma and die."

The woman stared at her, her gaze roving her body as if

she was looking for some outward sign. It would show up soon enough. Anna had only experienced it once and that was because of a mistake made by a camp counselor.

"Bullshit."

"Around my neck. There's a pendant. Look at it."

The woman set the drink down and reached into Anna's T-shirt and pulled out a silver chain with the words INSULIN DEPENDENT. TYPE 1 DIABETIC

"Well, don't you carry insulin on you?"

"Yes, I do, but the pack was in my mom's SUV."

"How do you know how high your blood sugars are?"

"I use a glucose meter but that was in there too."

"When was the last time you had insulin?"

She wasn't going to give her a specific time, but it was long enough that she would need insulin soon. Instead, she hoped by telling her that it was that morning, they might do as her mother said and decide to let her go.

She let the words hang out there, making the woman feel the gravity of the situation. The woman stared at her for a second, before yanking hard on the chain to get it to break away from her neck. Without another word said, she stormed out, not even closing the accordion door. Anna watched her exit the RV, yelling a name. "Bill! Bill!"

That was the first name she'd heard. Now all she needed was to put a face to the name.

As she waited, her eyes roamed the room and she plotted her escape.

10

Saratoga, New York

Bill squeezed the bridge of his nose upon hearing the news. Everything was going according to plan and now this. He couldn't believe it. He glanced down at his phone, searching for information, anything that he could use. Pam was in his face, almost hyperventilating. "What are we going to do? Huh? I told you this was not a good idea but you wouldn't listen to me."

Marcus chuckled. "See, Bill, this is what comes when you want to go all lone wolf on us. You should have listened. I say we cut her loose before this backfires even worse than it has already."

"Calm down," he said. Although inside he could feel his blood boiling, he couldn't let these two see that. He had to be the anchor, the steady one.

"He's right. C'mon, Bill, we don't need her," Pam said.

He got up from his folding seat. "No one is going anywhere. This is a bump in the road. Nothing more. How do you know she's even telling the truth?"

Pam tossed a necklace at him. "Look at it!"

"And? She could be lying."

He wasn't going to argue about it without verifying it for himself. Bill climbed a couple of steps into the RV, swiping his phone and reading an article. The moment he entered and caught sight of the girl, she stared at him with a defiant gaze, as if she'd bought herself a one-way ticket out of this. She hadn't. He hadn't come this far to see the rug pulled out from beneath him. Approaching, he let the pendant dangle in his hand as he stepped into the room.

"So, you're insulin-dependent. That true?"

"Why would I make it up?"

"Oh, I don't know, perhaps you think we'd show pity on you and leave you here while we drive off to find another one."

"Another one? So, you've done this before?"

He didn't answer. "The insulin. How long before you need it?"

"Immediately."

"When should you have had it?"

"An hour ago, maybe less."

"And what happens if you don't get it?"

"That's simple. I die."

He snorted, glancing back at the exit before looking at her. "You must think we're idiots." He showed her the screen of his phone. "Read that, can you? It says that you can survive for roughly three or four days without insulin."

"It varies. Not everyone is the same. Some will feel ill immediately while others will be in a daze for days. For some, it can take a while before they die, for others you are looking at forty-eight hours. It's not like we try this out to find out which one we fall into. But that's the least of your troubles because before then I'm going to get far worse. I'm talking really sick. You don't have any idea, do you? Look up hyperglycemia. It leads to a state called DKA. Do you want me to spell that out?" She was being cheeky but she was outraged and had every reason to be.

He wagged a finger in her face. "Don't push it!"

"I've already missed a dose. Once I start to get a dry mouth, I'll feel excessively thirsty, I'll get tired and confused. I'll get real sick, mister. I'll start getting shortness of breath, nauseated, and then throwing up begins. That's not a pretty sight."

"So, you vomit. Big deal."

"After that, I'll pass out and die," she bellowed. "And the speed of it occurring isn't just based on missing a meal, eating the wrong food, or not getting insulin, it can get worse even faster if I'm stressed. And right now, what do you think I am? So, unless you plan on leaving me somewhere, dropping me off at a hospital, or giving me back to my mother, it won't be long before you have a real problem on your hands," she barked, her anger surfacing.

"Shit," he spat. Bill snorted, head bobbing as he tried to get a grip on the situation. "All right. All right. Calm down. Until I can figure this out, what do you need right now?"

"To be released."

"Not happening."

"Water then. Lots of it. Wheat crackers too."

"And the insulin?"

"Lispro. The brand I use is Humalog. I don't know if I can take something else, I just know my mom says the dose is important, so make sure you get diabetic syringes. But best of luck getting it."

He nodded, making a mental note. Bill scrutinized her as he shifted his weight from one foot to the next, trying to maintain his cool and control over a situation that was quickly slipping through his fingers. *I've got this,* he told himself as he turned and headed out, slamming the door behind him.

"So?" Pam asked.

"Get back in there. Get her some water. Crackers too."

"We don't have any crackers."

"Then just keep an eye on her and give her water. I'll get some."

"But what are we doing about the insulin?"

"I'm thinking."

"Bill, you need to—"

As quick as a flash, Bill grabbed her by the hair and yanked her head back, his anger spilling over. "Are you hard of hearing?" His spit went in her face, a small amount trickling down the side of her cheek. Pam's nostrils flared and her eyes widened in fear. Lately, she'd been getting on his last nerve. Stepping over the line. Pushing the boundaries of her restricted freedom. He had a good mind to cut her loose but in some strange way, deep down, he enjoyed her company, that or controlling her. Bill shoved her toward the RV like a discarded toy. She stumbled, scrambling for the door like a wounded animal.

"You got something to add?" Bill asked Marcus.

He shook his head.

Marcus just stood there sneering, not saying a word. He wouldn't either. The last time he tried to intervene, he ended up with a black eye. Logic would have told them to leave but they had few things going for them, and despite Bill's tendency to fly off the handle from time to time, they knew where their bread was buttered. Better to side with the devil they knew than the devil they didn't.

Right then his burner phone rang. A glance at the caller ID, it was Rooster.

"Please tell me you have some good news."

"I'm in. Worked like magic," he said.

"Good. Keep it under control. You got it?"

"You know it. Look, uh, how come you never called?"

"Something came up."

"You had me nervous there for a moment. Bill, this only works if..."

Bill was quick to cut him off. "You don't need to tell me. I know." His harsh tone made it clear that he was in no mood to get a lecture. Rooster hung up and he turned to Marcus. "I need to go on a run to a pharmacy."

"They don't hand that shit out like candy, Bill. You need a prescription."

"Don't you think I know that? That's why you're coming with me."

"But what about the girl?"

"Pam can handle her. Hell, some days, I think she packs more balls than you," he said, making a beeline for the truck. The two of them got in and headed for a pharmacy in Saratoga Springs, sixteen minutes south. It was the closest and the only one that was open now that it was late. He switched on the headlights to full beam, a few cars honked their horn at him but Bill didn't bother to drop them. He stretched for his cigarettes, set one between his lips, and hit the truck lighter. A few seconds later it popped, and he scorched the end and blew smoke out the corner of his mouth. The ride was uneven due to the sheer number of birds that now littered the road.

"What do you make of all of this?"

Bill cut Marcus a side glance. "The birds?"

"No, the fish too."

"What are you talking about?"

Instead of explaining, Marcus leaned forward and turned on the radio. It didn't take more than a few taps of the button to land on a station that was talking about it.

"This is a major crisis we have on our hands."

"For sure, Doug, but it's not the first time we have seen this. Millions of fish washed up in Australia a few years back and it was discovered to be the result of blue-green algae. Red tides have also been a culprit. Then we have heatwaves. Our planet is going to experience some give and take. Maybe this is its way of taking."

"In one day? Come on, you can't be that naïve."

"Look, I'll admit it's strange, a mystery right now, but that was too when we first saw it. And that was soon ruled to be nothing more than a natural event. You've got to remember algae blooms; they are notorious for dropping the levels of oxygen too low for fish. That doesn't take into account fertilizers, automobiles, sewage, manure, and so on."

"But that's isolated. A one-off event. This has happened all over the globe."

"It's possible it could be the same."

"Then how do you explain the birds?"

"Well until they run some extensive tests, it could be the result of other forms of pollution."

"No, I don't buy that. Let's go ahead and take some phone calls from our listeners and hear what they have to say. We have Jill from Florida on the line. Hello Jill, you have the mic."

A moment passed then an angry caller came on the line.

"It's pretty obvious what this is, the government has been meddling again. They've been testing on animals for years. What's to say this isn't another one of their tests gone wrong? I wouldn't be surprised if they are the same people who assassinated Elvis Presley."

The host roared with laughter. "Thank you, Jill." They disconnected her before she could continue.

"Sounds like someone got out of the bed this morning wearing their tinfoil hat," the other radio host said with a laugh. "Next caller. Tim is from Texas. Let's hope you haven't been sucking down the Kool-Aid."

"Hey Doug, hey Jan, I love your show. Listen, I've been thinking about this all day. So, the birds fell first, right? Well, they landed in lakes, oceans, streams. What if something transferred? A disease that could cross from one species to another."

"Hmm, it's possible you might be onto something, Tim. Go on..."

"Well, I've been thinking, could this be some kind of lab-created bird flu? You know, like the Asian Avian Influenza." He became all excited. "I wouldn't be surprised if the Chinese are behind this shit. They've been gunning for us for years. They would love nothing more than to attack our great nation for the changes in tariffs. But I tell you this, Doug, if those bastards think they can pull the wool over this patriot's eyes, they have another thing coming. I've got an arsenal of guns in my house just waiting to go to war against..."

Click.

"And that was Tim from Texas. Let's hope this doesn't end up affecting Texas cattle or we could be looking at World War III, hey Jan," he said with a laugh.

"To be fair, Tim did raise a good point. The fish weren't reported dead until the birds hit the earth. I was doing some

research today about this, and I'm not sure our listeners know, but there were thousands of birds that fell in Arkansas years ago."

"Oh, please don't, Jan, you'll have people blaming this on white supremacists next." He burst out laughing. "Okay, moving on, who's our next caller?" A pause. "We have Benjamin Jones from North Carolina. Welcome to the show. What do you think?"

"Oh, it seems fairly simple to me," the man spoke in a thick Carolina accent. "I'm just a simple man but I got on my knees to pray today and the Lord showed to me a vision as clear as day."

"Wow, you must have a direct line as he's usually busy when I call," Doug replied in jest. "So, what did the big man have to say, Benjamin?"

"It's punishment for our sins. We've fallen away from him. Every one of us. We need to turn back. We need to repent. You see, God once wiped out humankind and saved the animals, this time he's decided to do the opposite."

Click.

"Well, even the almighty is getting blamed for this." Doug laughed. "What do you think, Jan, should we take one more?"

"Start like you mean to finish."

"We are suckers for punishment. Okay, next caller."

Bill switched it off. "Enough of that shit. None of that is going to help us."

"No, but it could work against us," Marcus said. "If this had only occurred in one town, or state, maybe people wouldn't be losing their shit, but people have been out all day panic buying. You should have seen some of the lines and fights taking place in the big cities. People believe this is the big one, Bill."

"People believe a lot of things. Listen to that last call. Most of its dumb shit perpetuated by idiots because they spent their life sucking on the teats of their mama's religion. Then you've got your conspiracy nuts and politicians looking for support in their next campaign. Look, life continues. We continue. Tomorrow these so-called experts will have some excuse, you'll see — an oil spill, chemtrails from planes flying high in the sky and leaving chemicals up there. We'll have a few rough months and we'll be back on our feet again ready to do the next dumb thing."

"Yeah, maybe, but that wasn't what they were discussing today," Marcus said. He never clarified and although Bill didn't want to feed into it, he couldn't help but be curious.

The drive shouldn't have taken more than twenty minutes tops but it had doubled with the sheer number of vehicles. Accidents. Emergency vehicles. Where was everyone heading? They had to travel on the hard shoulder just to avoid the slew of automobiles. They slowed to a crawl behind traffic and Bill had to ask. "All right. What were they discussing?" He blew smoke and tapped ash out the window as they veered around more vehicles that had been in accidents and left in the middle of the road because no tow trucks could get to all of them.

A few of the tow companies were out there but they had their work cut out for them. He hadn't seen this many collisions in his life.

"They think these mass animal deaths are related to some solar storm. That it's been messing up the magnetic force around the planet. That guy who mentioned the birds dying in Arkansas. That's only half the story. They also had over 100,000 drum fish wash up along the river. Either way, whatever has caused this, you can't deny what you're seeing," he said, motioning to lines of people hiking along the edge of the road, drivers, passengers, those coming from or going somewhere. The rest of the cars and trucks on the road were being cautious to avoid the slew of accidents.

"There's no telling what the repercussions will be from this," he said. "One thing is for sure, there's going to be a whole lot of people out of work, store owners, fishermen, those in the tourist business, and that will trickle down to hotels and supermarkets and we'll see price hikes on the rest of the food. And..."

Before Marcus could finish, they came down into the last stretch of road that would take them into the lot of the CVS pharmacy. Their eyes widened at the sight.

"Looting."

11

Vermont

It was a tangled mess of steel bones. Towing companies were the only ones benefiting from this disaster. It must have felt like Christmas day for them with an endless slew of vehicles stretching for miles along back roads, town streets, and major highways.

There was no way companies could handle it all.

Just as the police, fire, and ambulance services were overwhelmed, so were many others. It wasn't even like locals could help because if someone wasn't in a wreck, they knew of someone who was.

It was all hands on deck.

Every village, town, city. Like 9/11, this event's destructive power had left many in a daze, watching news reports, or trying to find their way out of the chaos.

If Travis had learned anything from the conversation with

Emily, it wasn't just birds hitting windshields or bouncing off the hoods that caused so many pile-ups, it was the reaction people would have had to avoid an accident. Some would swerve into other cars, others would slam on their brakes creating a collision, while still others would veer off the road into ditches, clipped by those speeding behind them.

The domino effect was astonishing.

Looking out down the strip of road, the carnage was both alarming and grotesque.

Bodies had been ejected out of windshields and open windows, others were trapped inside or under crumpled steel.

Still, a few brave EMTs were out there doing the best they could.

Blue and red strobe lights lit up the night.

A siren wailed from an ambulance as it worked its way through the maze of vehicles. It was one giant roadblock after another. "Look, we're not going to make it through here," Travis said. Kyle suggested returning to the previous exit. As he was doing a six-point U-turn he was starting to think this wasn't going to be as easy as he thought. He'd initially planned to hit Highway 279 west and then join NY-22 as it was a direct shot up to where Anna was on the map, but they'd been sitting in traffic for close to twenty minutes, crawling behind vehicles at a snail's pace only to see state troopers in the distance turning drivers around. Driving back, he slowed and brought his window down to speak with his brother.

"We're taking the back roads. How are you doing for gas?"

"I'll need to stop soon."

They had wanted to fill up in Eden Falls but the lineups were unreal as there were only two gas stations in town.

Returning to the off-ramp, Travis kept his truck on the

shoulder, navigating around off-kilter cars and trucks. Kyle continued every five minutes to use the police radio to get in contact with dispatch. It was a direct line but no one was answering. He figured if he could get through, they could notify local Albany police and perhaps get the jump on the kidnappers before it was too late.

"Something is not right. This system is flawless usually. They must have shut it down or switched to a backup system. This is unreal, in my sixteen years with the department I've never come across this."

"To be expected," Travis said with a nod to the endless array of emergencies surrounding them.

Sitting in the rear of the extended cab, Carla leaned forward between the seats. "I don't get it. It's been hours since they took her, and yet neither you nor Emily have heard any mention of a ransom. It doesn't make sense."

"Of course it does," Kyle piped up. "Not everyone abducts for money."

"Then what other reasons are there?"

Kyle didn't say. Travis knew as well as he did that there were only three reasons other than money, so he chimed in. "They either want to raise them, traffic them, or kill them."

Silence fell as his words lingered and images of the unthinkable sprang to mind. He'd been involved in two missing person cases in his time as a game warden. They were often called upon to help with search and rescue if the last known sighting was in a rural area. The first one had been a young mother, her body was found two months later by a hiker, and the second case involved two teenage girls. He'd been there when the search party discovered them. The sight of their bodies left a permanent imprint on his mind. In both cases, no one was brought to justice though many pointed fingers.

"Do you think they've done this before?" Carla asked.

It was hard to know if it was opportunistic or planned out. Though with the emergency lines tied up, it certainly opened the window for the worst of society to prey upon the weak. One look at the car wrecks and it was clear that many caught between a rock and a hard place would trust those around for help. Where others saw an opportunity to lend a hand, the low crustations of society saw a way to take advantage. "I hardly think it matters," Kyle replied.

"Well, it might give us some insight into who we're dealing with."

"Carla, this isn't one of your mystery shows. This is my daughter we're talking about," Kyle said.

"And she's my niece. I'm just baffled, that's all."

"We all are," Travis added.

"So why now?"

Kyle was starting to lose his patience. He sighed. "What are you talking about? Why now?"

"Well, is it because of this?"

"No. Not at all. Before this people were stealing kids off the streets. They don't need birds to rain down and fish to wash up to have a reason. Sure, maybe they've taken advantage of it but until we know more, who the hell knows." He huffed, running his palms across his pants and then squeezing them.

The tension between them was as clear as day. Like any sister, Carla would have Emily's back, especially after the way her relationship ended with Kyle, and he would show his distaste for her chiming in.

"So, you think the abduction was random?" she asked.

Kyle answered that. "I don't know, but it happens all the time." He shifted in his seat uncomfortably. It couldn't have been easy for him. His kid was out there, somewhere with strangers, animals that could have already harmed her. Travis was surprised Kyle hadn't fallen to pieces. Then again, in his line of work, he was paid to stay level-headed. It was the only way they could function.

"Doesn't seem random to me." Carla leaned back in her seat.

"Okay, expert. And why might that be?" Kyle asked if only so he could shoot down her theory.

"Broad daylight. On a highway. You say abductions occur all the time but how often like that?"

"I wouldn't know, Carla, maybe you can ask them when we see them."

"Do you think they know you?"

Kyle twisted in his seat, his face contorting. "What are you insinuating?

"Well, it's no mystery you've made your fair share of enemies in this town."

Travis eyed her in his mirror. He could sense she wanted to say more. She opened her mouth and then closed it, opting to look out the window. It was a good point though, both he and Kyle had knocked heads with all manner of people. If they couldn't get at them, what better way than to target a relative? Still, though, it seemed a little out there that someone local would travel to Albany to kidnap Anna. There were countless times they could have taken her and they would have been none the wiser. Everything about the brazen nature in which they scooped her up in broad daylight on a major highway suggested they were either following her or opportunistic. Either way, it was a sick move to pull.

"I think you're forgetting yourself," Kyle muttered.

Carla took offense to that. "And by that you mean?"

"You haven't exactly been running around with the best crowd. It's common to find addicts in debt to dealers."

"Is that so?"

"And if I remember right, a year ago, Emily pulled you out of a crack house upstate."

"I entered rehab."

"Yeah, three times."

She leaned forward and with one glare Travis felt the atmosphere change.

"So, I've fallen off the wagon a few times. We've all got vices. At least I'm trying. From what Emily shared with me, you never got back on."

"What you've heard and what is true are two different things."

"Is that what you tell yourself? You know, Kyle, the first of the twelve steps is honesty, most struggle to get past that because they live in denial." She tapped him on the shoulder and sank back into her seat with a grin as she began listing the next eleven. She was alluding to Kyle's heavy drinking, the very thing that had been the fuel of many of the arguments in his defunct marriage.

Kyle narrowed his gaze and turned on the radio. Traffic. News. Music. He scanned through the stations seemingly with no other reason than to tune out Carla. Travis scooped up his phone and checked his messages to see if Emily had sent him anything. She said she would update him if there was any movement, any change of direction.

Nothing.

He glanced at the GPS and the destination of Saratoga.

They drove for another ten minutes, cutting through the countryside near the edge of a two-lane road. There was talk about what they would do when they arrived, but Travis had a sense that they would deal with that when it came to it.

First, they needed gas.

It didn't take long to find an out-of-the-way, rundown gas station. It was set back from the road; a rusted Exxon sign blew in the wind as a light rain continued to fall. The station was small, with a cashier and several aisles of snacks. Even in the backcountry, there was a line, though here only three other cars were vying to use the two pumps. Travis waved Danny ahead of them and he slid into a spot and killed the engine.

Carla scrambled out. "I'm getting something to eat."

"Can you get me a pack of smokes?" Kyle said.

"Get them yourself," Carla replied.

As Travis inserted the nozzle of the pump, the wind blew rain in his face, making the whole experience even more miserable. Danny remained quiet filling his tank. Kyle got out and stretched his legs while Carla entered the station and began browsing.

As gasoline gushed into the truck, his mind circled the comments between Kyle and Carla. Both of them had raised valid points. There had been no mention of a ransom so was this a spur-of-the-moment decision or some kind of payback? Travis went through the Rolodex of his mind thinking of anyone who might have wanted to get back at Emily or him. Of course, Kyle would have been the obvious choice but this was his daughter. What would he have to gain? He glanced at Carla inside. She certainly had knocked heads with Emily as of late, especially after being told to leave, but even for her, this would be extreme. His eyes circled to Danny. He didn't want to entertain that thought. He had a lot of reasons to want Travis to feel pain. He'd lost his wife and child and though he hadn't said it directly, in a roundabout way it was clear he blamed Travis.

No. It was stupid. There was nothing to be gained. The stress of everything that had happened today was beginning to wear on him and play with his mind.

The gasoline pump made a clunking sound on the other side as Danny finished up and went into the station and asked the owner if he could use the bathroom. Kyle had bought a pack of cigarettes and passed him on the way out. He lit one and then leaned up against the truck, looking up at the dreary night of rain.

"Smoking around a gasoline pump. Not smart," Travis said, removing the nozzle.

"Neither is inviting those two along but we all make mistakes," he replied without looking at him. Travis shook his head as he went inside. Carla came out with a pile of snacks, drinks, and a magazine. For someone worried about her niece, she didn't look too concerned.

At the counter, waiting behind one other patron, Travis lifted his eyes to a flatscreen TV. It wasn't loud but it was easy to get the gist of the story. The news streamed clips of dead fish and birds all over the earth. There were whales, dolphins, and every type of fish being dragged in by fishermen, eager to save what they could.

Was it salvageable?

He wouldn't be thinking that but large corporations hell-bent on pocketing money would, even if it meant serving up sea life that could now be harmful to society.

"Crazy, right?" the young cashier said. "I swear this is some end-times shit."

Travis nodded, tossed a few bills on the counter, and told him which pump. Out the corner of his eye, he saw Carla lingering around Danny's bike.

"What do you think?"

"What?" he asked looking back at the clerk, distracted.

"Do you believe what they're saying?"

"I don't know, what's new?"

The guy laughed, handing him his change. "Seriously, every person who has come into this store tonight has asked me about this but you look as if your mind is elsewhere."

"It is," he said, turning away.

As he went to head out, Danny came back in with the key to the bathroom. He was on the phone talking to someone, his head low. "You're to wait for my arrival."

He almost bumped into him. He glanced up and got this look of shock on his face, quickly hanging up.

"You good?" Travis asked.

"Yeah." He tossed the key to the cashier. "Thanks, man."

"Who was that on the phone?"

"A friend."

Travis headed out and Carla stepped away from Travis' bike and prepared to get into the truck. "You know how to ride?" Travis asked Carla.

"No, just didn't want to sit in the truck with him," she muttered before climbing in. Kyle caught what she said and snorted, tossing his finished cigarette out the window.

After strapping in, they peeled away from the gas station. The roads were slick, dark, in some areas there weren't any lights. Bringing down his window to clear the air of the rank smell of tobacco, Travis could hear the throaty buzz of Danny's bike behind as it picked up speed. He eyed his brother in the side mirror, wondering if their relationship would ever be the same.

They hadn't been on the road for more than ten minutes when, out the corner of his eye, he saw the motorcycle wipeout.

It was like watching a racing accident, the back end went out from underneath him and shot across the roadway while he went into a full-body tumble, spinning over and flipping in the air like a rag doll only to land on the edge of the road.

Travis slammed the brakes on and the back end of his truck fishtailed.

"What the hell," Carla said, nearly spilling a can in the back.

Travis spun the wheel and did a U-turn in the road and sped back, hoping, praying that his brother was alive.

12

Vermont

Heavy rain beat against the windowpane as Rooster scooped up the remains of the chili in his bowl with one final swipe of bread. He tapped it in the air before devouring it in one bite. "Damn, that was outstanding. I haven't had a meal that good since I was a kid. What's the secret?" He followed up by reaching for a bottle of Budweiser and downing the remainder.

"Well, thank you," Steph replied, wiping the corner of her lip and trying to answer with her mouth full of food. "The key is to work the chili powder into the meat as you brown it, don't add too many tomatoes which will overpower it, and then add some beer."

"I'll have to come back here more often."

Lucas grinned at her, observing the two of them like a ball being tossed back and forth over a tennis net.

She got up and offered Rooster some more but he declined. He'd already had two bowls. Steph carried the dishes to the sink and let them soak in a bowl of suds while she collected a blueberry pie from the fridge. It was rare for her to allow guests into her main kitchen. They usually ate in a separate dining area but as he was the only guest, she didn't like the idea of him eating alone especially after he'd gallantly come to her aid.

"So where did the nickname Rooster come from?" she asked over her shoulder.

"When I was a kid, I used to get up early and make a ruckus. My mother would tell her friends she didn't use an alarm clock because she had a rooster."

Steph laughed.

He winked at Lucas who seemed to be enjoying his company. It was certainly taking his mind off the situation. She was hoping that her brother would phone with news. "So, you mentioned your brother is from Burlington, is that right?"

He nodded.

"Must be difficult living so far away?"

"Ah, no, I get up there quite a lot. What about you? You got family?"

"Two brothers. Both here in Eden Falls."

"No husband?"

She finished cleaning the dishes and set them on the counter to dry before drying her hands. "Once. He passed away. Aneurysm."

There was an awkward beat.

"I'm sorry to hear that."

"It was a long time ago."

He got up and strolled over, getting uncomfortably close

to her. "You missed some," he said, taking the dishcloth and wiping the back of her arm where there were soap suds. "I'd imagine any man would be proud to have you as their wife." It was an odd comment to make. She put some distance between herself and him by walking over to the fridge and taking out some whipped cream. "Dessert?"

"Sounds delicious. So, tell me, you run this place all by yourself?"

She nodded, taking out some plates.

"That's right."

"No staff in the mornings?"

"Nope. Just me. I've thought about getting a cleaner in but, and maybe it's an inability to let go of control, I'm not sure I could leave what I can do myself in the hands of someone else. It seems to me where inns fail is in the small details, and a cleaner working on minimum wage isn't going to give this place the care and attention that I would."

"Very resourceful. Don't leave things in the hands of others. I'm all about that too. I like to get my hands dirty."

"Yeah? What do you do for a living, Mr. Shepard?"

He waved her off. "Ah, call me Rooster." He paused and leaned back against the kitchen counter, watching her cut the pie. "You could say I'm a general laborer. I do the work that others won't do. A bit of everything."

"A jack of all trades," she added.

He laughed, crossing his feet and stretching. "That would be it."

Steph brought over the plates and he returned to his seat at one end of the table as she did the same. "Forgive me for asking, but the boy doesn't look like you?"

"No, he's my brother's girlfriend's son. Lucas."

"Hmm," he said, then scooped some of the pie into his

mouth. "So, they went out for the evening? Or are they working?"

She paused, a fork hovering a few inches away from her mouth. She didn't want to disturb him with the details. Enough was happening around them right now that bringing something as personal as this into the mix wouldn't help the situation. Instead, she opted to shift the conversation away. "Would you like another beer?" It was easier that way. A phone rang and she instinctively looked at hers but it was Rooster's. He took it out of his pocket, still chewing pie, and answered it.

"Hello."

She collected a beer and set it in front of him.

"No, everything is good. The company is wonderful," he said looking at her. "Yeah. The Wilson House Inn. That's right." He nodded. "I know, brother, and I will see you soon too." He hung up. She noticed that he'd been on the phone three times in two hours already. "Family," he said. "What we do for our kin, right?"

She nodded.

The remaining conversation was light and circled her. He was very inquisitive about the town, her life, her brother but specifically about Emily's sister.

"I've met her a couple of times but from what I've heard she has quite the colorful past," Steph said.

"Sounds like it. Do you know her well?"

"No."

Steph nodded and studied him as he took another scoop of pie.

"So, with your brother being a game warden, I expect he had something to say about this event."

"Not yet. No. Though I'm sure there's a very good explanation."

"Birds falling. Fish washing up. What do you think they'll say?" Rooster asked.

"I don't speculate neither do I rule anything out. All things are possible."

He smiled.

As they were finishing up, Steph heard a knock at the door. She rose from the table and excused herself. Making her way down the hardwood corridor, beyond the glass she could see the silhouette of someone. They banged against the door again.

"All right. All right. I'm coming."

Steph pulled it open and squinted at a figure who was wearing a fishing jacket with a large hood. Rain poured off the edge. "I heard you have room for one more," he said, lifting his head to meet her gaze. Steph's eyes widened at the sight of the same man who'd stolen her bag in the parking lot. She shifted back fast and tried to slam the door but he pushed his foot into the gap, stopping it short of closing. A quick shove and Steph fell onto her butt. Shuffling back, the stranger entered, closing the door behind him.

"Rooster!" Steph yelled.

The man was holding a gun on her, a grin flickering on his face. She scrambled to her feet and raced into the kitchen only to find Rooster with his arm around Lucas' throat and the tip of a gun pressed against his head. "I see you've met my brother. Bernard."

Her head turned back and forth as the man approached wielding his pistol. He nudged her into the kitchen. She wanted to grab up Lucas but Rooster wouldn't let her come near him.

"Let him go!"

"Ah come now, Steph. Calm down. Let's not ruin things. We've had such a pleasant evening."

"He's just a kid."

"And he'll remain that way for now."

"What do you want?" she asked, her gaze bouncing between them.

Rooster kept a firm hand on Lucas. "That's simple. Just a bed for the night, and the company of you two."

She scrutinized them both. "You're with them, aren't you? The ones who took Anna?"

Rooster smiled and pointed at her. "You're catching on fast. Now come on, take a seat." When she didn't move fast enough, his calm smiling demeanor shifted. "SIT!" he bellowed. Bernard shoved her toward the table. Slowly, she sat. All the while Lucas wiggled in Rooster's grasp. "Stop moving, kid!" he said into his ear. "Unless you want to see my brother here hurt your auntie. Come to think of it, you aren't his auntie." He chuckled and then made Lucas sit in a chair. Bernard tossed some zip ties to Rooster and he used them to secure Lucas to the chair. Bernard did the same with her.

Rooster returned to his seat.

"There. Much better. Now, where were we?"

He collected the beer she'd gotten out for him and twisted off the cap. Bernard picked at the food on the table. "Bernard. Where're your manners?"

He picked up a knife, stuck it in a piece of bread, brought it up to his goatee, and took a bite. He was a foul-looking man. Long, slick hair and a pitted face with dark circles under the eyes. Beneath the long, black fishing trench coat he wore a red plaid shirt and dark jeans. He stank like cigarettes and alcohol. "Go around to the doors, make sure they're locked, and bring all the blinds down. We don't want any lookie-loos, now do we?" Rooster grinned as he took a seat.

"Why are you doing this?" She asked.

Without answering he continued to eat his pie with a smile lurking at the corners of his lips.

MILES AWAY IN NEW YORK, Emily glanced at the charge on the phone. How much power was left in the watch? She'd forgotten to ask. She'd dropped the brightness and turned off any apps running in the background, and set the iPhone to low power mode. Under the cover of night, her face illuminated by the phone, she stared at iMessage waiting for a text from Anna. She'd checked the car to see if there was a charger, but there wasn't. She wouldn't wait until it was too low before she found one.

A prevailing thought pushed through that if she wasn't so busted up, she could have given chase.

But realistically, how far would she have gotten alone?

The faces of the man and woman flashed in her mind.

She wracked her brain, wondering if she'd seen them before. She wanted to contact Travis and get an update, but there was nothing he could tell her. He was trying to get there as fast as he could. She was scared. Alone. And in doubt about the outcome. These things rarely worked out. Twenty-four hours was being generous in an abduction case. More times than not a kid only stayed alive a few hours. Except Anna wasn't just any kid. She was strong, resilient, smart but also suffering from diabetes and that put the odds of her survival even lower.

If she died or was murdered, Emily wasn't sure what she

would do. Her kids were her life. The very reason she had walked out on a bad marriage after fourteen years.

Had her abductor known them?

Kyle had warned her to be vigilant, to be on the lookout for anything out of place. *I will make enemies. It comes with this line of work.* He wasn't paranoid about it but he often reminded her. *If you see anything unusual let me know.* When they would go to a restaurant he would never sit with his back to the exit. Kyle always had to be at the rear of the restaurant, closer to the back doors, where he had a good view of everyone. To others, it must have seemed weird, especially friends when they went out for a meal, but she'd just gotten used to it.

That was back when things were good.

How had everything gone so wrong? It wasn't like she hadn't fought for her marriage. Kyle wasn't a bad person but he'd changed over the years. Become withdrawn. She thought it was his work. Coming home, reaching for a beer the moment he walked in the door, slumping in a chair, and expecting his meal to be just right or he would start an argument. He never seemed to have enough gas in his tank to talk and when she tried, she just got her head bitten off.

If it was just that alone, she might have let it slide, notched it up to a bad season, a bad year even, but it just gradually got worse to where his drinking was affecting the kids. He'd snap at them and refuse to spend time with the family.

And then there was that day.

When he lifted his fist at her. She knew it was over right then. He didn't need to hit her to know that what they had was gone. Like many other women in the same position, she wondered if she was to blame, wondered whether she was jumping the gun. He blamed the drink and perhaps it was, but by the third time it happened, she no longer had the energy to care.

A few days later he finally followed through with the threat and struck her.

Fortunately, that night, the cops were called out by neighbors, but unfortunately, he managed to avoid them arresting him. He had said that it was nothing more than a spat.

The bruise under her eye the next day proved that wrong.

With evidence they couldn't deny, they had to look at it again.

That's when that evening's police report was called into question.

The extent of police work by his colleagues amounted to sending him elsewhere for the night and then filing a report that was heavily in favor of him. Calling her erratic. Unhinged even. She was far from that. She came to learn that was often how departments dealt with domestic matters. Her lawyer had told her clearer than anyone else. "Officers who are guilty of domestic violence are rarely fired, arrested or prosecuted." In his case, he was placed on restricted duties, and within a few weeks was back out in the community.

Still, somewhere deep inside she thought there was hope for her marriage, and like a fool, she gave him one more chance until it happened again.

This time he was suspended without pay for eighty hours and forced to go through some remediation training on domestic violence. Still, they never took his job.

The thought that he might do the same to the kids ate away at her, and after one more week, and summoning enough courage and help from two close friends, she planned to leave. But instead, he opted to leave the house. She would have left herself but didn't have anywhere to go with the kids and she figured he wanted to act like he was doing it for their benefit.

A day later, she followed up by filing a case against him, which had led to the court awarding her temporary custody. As for love, well, she deserved better and she'd found that in Travis. He wasn't a saint. Far from it. He had his own baggage but it was a far cry from Kyle's. They'd known each other a while, worked alongside each other as the Fish & Game Department called in biologists to help. While she never cheated on Kyle, she did start seeing Travis before the divorce was officially finalized. Her lawyer had warned her against it but by the time she got the advice, it was too late.

Emily wiped tears away.

Get a grip.

She cracked open the rear door and shuffled off into the inky night to search for a working car and a charger that might fit the iPhone.

13

"She's no good to me dead," Bill said, tucking a Glock 22 in the back of his jeans after getting out of the truck. The CVS Pharmacy was a chaotic scene, as people rushed in and out taking whatever they wanted.

"But what if the cameras record us? All this would be for nothing."

"Listen, you idiot. The last thing on anyone's mind right now is identifying looters. Do you see any cops?"

He looked around and shook his head.

"And you won't. They are too busy. Now let's go."

They hurried toward the red brick building. Carts clattered outside, as giddy-eyed locals pillaged the building, carrying out as much as they could with armfuls of boxes and shopping bags. Inside, a deafening alarm rang out. Store workers had given up trying to stop people. He saw one dash out in full uniform. The minimum wage didn't offset the risk factor. "I'll take that too," one woman said to the cashier cowering behind the counter. She took out a rack of gift cards under one arm while another guy behind the counter was using a baseball bat to threaten a woman to open the cash register.

"Open it now bitch, if I have to ask again, I'm going to crush your skull."

She didn't need to be convinced. The clerk took some card, swiped the machine, and pressed a few buttons. It dinged, and hey presto it was open. The thug howled, feasting his eyes upon the green and pulling wads of it out, and stuffing it in his pockets. "Much obliged."

Bill hurried past the almost bare shelves that lined the aisles, product was all over the floor. A man ahead was scooping large armfuls into his cart while rolling forward. Bill dashed past him and was almost knocked over by several others crossing the other way. They made a beeline for the meds in the back but were already too late. Hopping over the counter, they were met by the sight of more bare shelves.

To addicts, it had been an absolute gold mine.

The few things that remained were general pills. Still, that didn't stop him from looking. Marcus yelled, "Bill, over here." Hope vanished when he saw Marcus standing in front of a table where an Indian pharmacist in a white lab coat was cowering beneath.

Bill dropped to a crouch. "Diabetes. Insulin. I need some and syringes."

He stuttered. "I... I... I don't..."

Before he could form the words, Bill put a meaty hand on him and yanked him out, slamming him up against the wall. He brought a gun up under his chin. "Point me in the direction of diabetes medication. Now!" He pointed and Marcus hurried across to check while he kept the gun on him.

"It's empty. Shit. Do you not have a storage area? Extra supplies?"

The man shrugged. Bill lost his cool and pistol-whipped him, knocking him to the ground where he continued to beat the side of his skull until Marcus pulled him off. "Enough. That isn't getting us anywhere. There's a pharmacy in the Walmart and a Walgreens not far from here."

A few gunshots rang out near the front of the store.

Several women screamed. "All right," he replied, following Marcus out but keeping his gun by his side. He wouldn't hesitate to use it. On the way back to the truck, he saw one person lying in a pool of blood, and another clutching his chest, with a gun still in hand. He'd been in riots before, protests that had turned violent in the Big Apple, but the population there was over eight million, here it was less than twenty-seven thousand. If people were losing their shit in small towns, this event was hitting harder than he thought. Sprinting back to the truck, he couldn't help but wonder how this would all play out. Meanwhile, it only increased the need to get this matter dealt with fast.

Back inside the truck, he spun wheels as he screamed out of the lot, almost crashing into two vehicles. The streets were madness, they weren't absent of cops but there weren't enough to deal with this. He saw their lights in the distance, and several cops hauling people into cruisers, but they were up against far more than they could deal with. One city, one state even, and they could wrangle it back into order, but an entire country or the globe? The world had already been teetering on the edge of losing their shit when this happened. Protests, riots, school shootings, viral outbreaks, it was a disaster and now with this, it felt like hell had opened up to swallow the rest of them.

Maybe his fears were getting the better of him.

He wasn't like Marcus, swayed by every news article. Sure,

it was odd, but what were they meant to do? Wait for it to blow over? The opportunity had presented itself and he'd taken it. Now it was just a matter of keeping the girl alive long enough to get paid.

Hurtling up the road, they weaved through the streets, avoiding traffic until they made it to Walmart. From the moment they arrived at the pharmacy, they knew it was a bust. Windows were shattered, and the shelves were bare. Ten minutes later, they were at Walgreens and staring at more of the same.

"Shit." He slammed his fist against the counter.

Marcus looked at him with those "I told you so" accusing eyes.

He dropped to a crouch, bringing both hands to the side of his head and willing his heart to slow down.

"What now?" Marcus asked.

"Nothing else to do but make the call."

THE MOTORCYCLE WAS a complete write-off but fortunately, his brother's leather gear, though badly torn, had saved him from what could have been fatal. He was lying there not moving, so Travis had rushed over thinking he was dead. "Danny!"

Danny groaned, turning onto his back.

"Are you…?"

"Don't even ask." He screwed up his face and groaned as he sat up. Kyle and Carla were out and making their way over.

"What the hell happened?" Travis asked.

"Beyond the obvious?" He coughed hard and winced. "The damn engine seized, the rear wheel locked and bumped me off. Makes no sense." With a confused look, he gazed at his bike that was a crumpled mess in the ditch. He groaned, moving his head from side to side, and holding his left arm. He got up and removed his motorcycle gloves. The helmet was scratched, even cracked slightly, but still in one piece. Danny arched his back. "Damn that hurt."

"How would that happen?" Travis asked.

"Overheating, a lack of lubrication, I don't know," he said, slowly making his way over to the bike. "I topped up the oil before I came out today, so it can't be that." Danny bent down over the bike and unscrewed the dipstick, wiped it in the grass, and inserted it again to see how much oil was inside. Once he removed it, he squinted. "What the hell?"

It was beyond low; the stick was barely showing any oil.

"A leak," Travis said.

"If it was leaking, I would have noticed."

"At night?"

"This is almost bone dry. That's impossible." He felt around the underside of the bike then withdrew his hand covered in oil. "Well, that explains it, the oil drain plug is gone." Travis turned and looked at Carla. He'd seen her close to the bike, examining it. But she had no reason to touch it nor would Kyle. Besides, whoever had done this would have needed a wrench.

"Is it possible the plug was loose?"

"I guess but... I only stopped at your house and the gas station, that was it."

Danny looked at them all, Travis included. "The main thing is you're alive."

"Yeah," Danny said unconvinced as he staggered past them, with a hand on his elbow, heading for the truck. Travis stood there for a moment looking at the bike before returning. He removed gear from the rear of the cab and tossed it into the bed of the truck to make room for Danny. He climbed in, grimacing.

"He should get that arm looked at," Carla said.

"I'll drop you off at the hospital," Travis offered.

"We can't go back, there's no time," Danny said.

Kyle added, "We're still in Vermont. Southwestern is the closest."

"Don't remind me," Danny said.

Travis glanced at his phone. There had been no text from Emily. No news was good news. But this was the last thing they needed. He was beginning to regret agreeing to let them come. "You're injured."

"I'm fine," Danny said dismissively as he winced with every move he made. Carla touched his arm and he wailed.

"Doesn't sound fine to me," Carla said.

"You're no good with a busted arm," Travis added.

"He's right," Kyle agreed. "Besides, you could have internal injuries."

"Whatever. Let's go." He waved them on.

Travis looked over at Kyle and he shrugged while getting back in the passenger side. As they headed back, Carla remained quiet, staring out the window. Danny looked back at his wrecked bike, shaking his head.

THE WENCH, as Anna liked to refer to her, had placed two large glasses of water in her room, and stepped outside for a smoke. She'd pulled the accordion pocket door closed and told her that Bill had gone to collect some insulin. With her wrists and ankles still bound together, Anna shuffled across the bed and pushed up the blinds on the window to get a better look at where she was.

Hey Siri, send a text to my mom.

What do you want to say? Siri came back.

I'm in an RV park. I can't see a sign but it's a park.

Saratoga RV Park. That's the only one near your location, her mother replied.

Pam was sitting on the folding chair, smoking a cigarette. She never mentioned where the young guy Marcus had gone. Was he out there? Had he gone with Bill? A text came back in. *Are you alone?* her mom asked.

There's only one of them here, I think. She's outside.

Can you see a way out?

There are two windows.

She tried to see if they would unlock but one of them wouldn't even budge. The second one on the other side of the bedroom opened but only partially. It was stiff, rusted and without her hands free she would have made one hell of a ruckus trying to get out.

What about people. Can you see people?

With the windows open she could see shapes in the distance but couldn't hear anyone. *There are people in the distance but there's no way they could hear me without her hearing me first.*

What about a signal. Do you have a flashlight nearby?

She remembered Pam walking out of the room and lighting a cigarette inside the RV, setting the cigarettes and lighter on the counter before closing the door. If she could get that lighter. *Hold on mom, let me try something.*

She swung her feet off the bed and shuffled over to the door that separated the bedroom from the rest of the RV. A quick tug, she expected it to be locked. It wasn't. Before she acted, she hopped to the window and lifted the blinds. Pam was still there, looking off into space, half a cigarette remained.

Moving as fast as she could without falling over, Anna shuffled through the opening of the accordion door over to the counter. She was a few feet away when she heard the door open.

Anna froze, expecting any second for Pam to enter.

But she didn't. The door closed again and she heard her walk away.

Staying still, she listened before quickly snagging up the lighter and hopping back into the room. As she did, she passed the washroom and noticed a can of air freshener inside. An idea sprang to mind. A year ago, Lucas had gotten into trouble with one of his friends for playing around with a lighter and an aerosol can. He said it was a school project and that he was trying to create a homemade flame thrower. Their mother didn't believe him and grounded him for a week. She'd seen it in action, the flame it kicked out. Now a small lighter, that might not get someone's attention, but a large flame... Anna grabbed it up and made her way back into the bedroom. She closed the door behind her and worked her way around the bed to the window on the opposite side of the RV to Pam.

Before trying what she had in mind, she needed to get the lighter flame near the spray area. The difficulty was holding the lighter in one hand, and the aerosol in the other. She fumbled around with it and dropped the can twice before realizing she could rub the plastic portion of the zip tie against the edge of the window and cut right through it.

Shifting it back and forth, she would stop every few seconds just to listen.

No footsteps. She hadn't heard.

Again, she started, working the plastic hard against the metal frame until finally, it snapped and her hands came loose. "Yes."

Not wasting a second, she took the lighter and burned through the plastic around her ankles until they were free.

Next, Anna leaned out the window, taking both arms and holding them as far out as she could before she let a burst of hot orange light up the night.

Once, twice, three times she did it then waited.

Had they seen it? Figures in the distance moved but no one came her way. She did it again but on the second try, she heard the door open on the RV. Acting fast, she got under the covers of the bed and waited.

Pam opened the door. "Are you tired?"

"Just a little."

"Well..." as she was about to say something, Pam's gaze went to the window. "Did you open that?" She came charging around and was in the process of closing it and yelling at her when Anna pulled out the lighter and can, and unleashed a foot-long flame. It caught alight Pam's thin T-shirt, turning the whole thing into a fiery mess.

Pam screamed.

She slapped the can out of her hand and went for her but Anna bounced out of that bed, rolled off the other side, and picked up the can. Not more than a second later she unleashed another flame at her. She didn't let up on the spray nozzle this time as she backed out of the room. Pam's screams of anguish only increased as she rolled on the bed to put out the flames.

That was her moment.

Her one chance to run.

Anna turned and burst out of the RV into the night.

Heart pounding in her chest, frantic to get away, she just made a beeline for RVs in the distance. She could see the lights through the trees, a fire outside. "Help!" Behind her, she heard Pam coming after her. She looked over her shoulder, panting hard, crying out for help, anyone that would hear her, only to slam into someone.

But before she could breathe a sigh of relief, she looked up to see it was Bill.

A hand clamped over her mouth. He hoisted her up as if she didn't weigh more than a feather and charged back over to the RV, scowling at Pam as he passed her. "You and I will have words," he said. "But first you." Bill looked down at her in a terrifying manner.

14

Due to accidents on the road, they hadn't even made it out of Vermont, and with Southwestern Vermont Medical Center the closest, turning back to the hospital made sense even if it did add on an extra thirty minutes. The plan was to drop him off and then continue without him. What they didn't realize was that every hospital was inundated with accident victims. The parking lot was so packed that Travis had to swing into the emergency lane which was dedicated to ambulances. Strobe lights were flashing, lighting up the night as he put the truck in park, and got out to help him.

By now the adrenaline had worn off, and the pain had ramped up. Danny cradled his left arm, moaning as he got out.

"I'll take him in," Carla said. "Don't leave without me."

"Okay, hurry up," Travis said.

"Sorry, brother," Danny added.

He shrugged and shook his head as he watched Carla lead him through double doors.

Kyle breathed in deeply. "You know, Travis, the roads are a mess. You could stay here with your brother. Carla and I can handle this."

Travis' brow furrowed. He answered him without looking at him. "I'm not staying."

"I'm just saying."

"Yeah, well don't."

"Fine." Kyle leaned forward, casting a glance off toward the hospital. "Don't you find it a little odd? What happened back there to your brother?"

"It was an accident."

"I'm talking about your brother's response to a seized-up engine. I don't know about you, but most guys who ride motorcycles give it their due diligence. He knew when to fuel up but not to check his oil? C'mon."

"What are you getting at? It was an accident."

"You can't be that blind."

"To what?"

"Carla."

Travis looked back at the hospital. He could see Carla speaking with a nurse through the glass. "You think she had something to do with it?"

"Well, don't you?"

"No. She barely knows Danny. She was the one who wanted to come with us and help. What reason would she have to slow us down or cause an accident?"

"I don't know. That's the same question I've been asking myself since I saw her poking around his bike at the gas station."

"Did you see her do something?"

"No, but..."

He was about to respond when Emily phoned him to get

an update. His heart sank at the thought of telling her that they weren't even close to leaving. Travis lifted a finger to Kyle and mouthed the words, hold that thought. He didn't think Carla was involved but it was odd. Danny was no amateur. He cared for that bike like it was his wife. He'd been riding for years.

"Hey, hon..." before he could finish Emily was already on him.

"You nearly there?"

Travis squeezed the bridge of his nose. "Far from it. Look, the roads are bad, we already had to take one detour, and now something's cropped up but we'll be back out there in a few minutes."

"Cropped up? Back out there? What are you talking about? Where are you?"

"Vermont. The hospital."

"Vermont? Travis."

He brought her up to speed and naturally, fearful for her Anna, she unleashed her frustration. He stepped away, noticing that Kyle was lingering, trying to listen to the conversation. "Look, I'm doing the best I can. I didn't expect this to happen. He's my brother."

"And she's my daughter."

"If he's got internal bleeding, he could die, Emily."

"If she doesn't get insulin, she will die." She exhaled hard. "Hell, she could be dead already. She was trying to alert people nearby; I haven't heard from her since. She's not answering."

"Answering. You contacted her?"

"By iMessage."

"Emily. You could have put her in danger. The watch gives off a notification sound."

"She said it didn't. So that setting I changed in Sound and Haptics must have worked. It's only using haptic vibration."

"But still."

"Look, I'm not going to argue. I was able to find out there are three of them holding her. She's in an RV and right now that RV is parked in Saratoga RV Park. But for how much longer I don't know." Travis looked over to the truck. She began to cry, blaming herself. "I shouldn't have taken her with me. I should have just..."

"Hey. Hey, stop! Don't do that. C'mon now. We'll get to her. I'm leaving. If Anna replies, let me know what she says. Find out some names. Maybe we can figure out who these people are and what they want." As he was speaking with her, he looked over to the truck and Kyle's phone rang as Carla was coming out of the hospital.

"Look, I gotta go."

He hung up and made his way over.

"All good?" Travis asked Carla.

She blew out her cheeks. "Your brother is stubborn. He doesn't want to stay but I managed to get a nurse to speak to him. He'll have a long wait, that's for sure. You should see it, it's crazy inside there. Tons of people. All of them are in the same or worse state. The nurse said he'll be lucky if someone gets to him by tomorrow."

Travis sighed. He was torn. Taking him to another hospital in a smaller town might work but there was no time for that. "All right, jump in," he said. As Carla got in, she tossed her open backpack from one side to the other. As she did that, something clattered inside and Travis caught a glint of silver. "What the hell...?" he said as he reached into the bag and withdrew a wrench that was partially covered in oil.

He looked at her, and she frowned, a look of confusion spreading. "That's not mine."

"So, why's it in there?"

Noticing, Kyle wrapped up his phone call and pointed at it. "Sonofabitch."

Carla shook her head. "No. No. I didn't do it."

"So you always carry a wrench covered in oil around with you?" Kyle asked.

"That's not mine. I just told you."

"Then explain," Travis barked.

"I don't need to explain anything to you."

"Get out of the truck," Kyle said.

"Why? I didn't do anything. Why would I?"

"I don't know, maybe one of your drug friends told you to do it. The same ones that have taken Anna?" Kyle said. "Perhaps that's why you're here, to keep track of us, make sure they stay one step ahead."

"Fuck you. That's my niece you're talking about. I would never harm her."

"That's not what I heard," Kyle said. "Lucas told me you and Emily had a big fight and were yelling. He said you were pissed at Emily for tossing you out because Emily found drugs in the house, drugs that could have been found by my kids, by our kids. That's why she wants you gone. You're a danger to them."

"And you're not? You are so full of shit, man! You want to point the finger. Go ahead. How about you? Huh? The threats you made to Emily."

"What happened between me and her is our business. I was drinking back then. We might not see eye to eye as a couple but neither she nor I would put our kids in danger."

"Is he telling the truth?" Travis asked. This was news to

him. Not the part about Kyle being an asshole. He knew about that from Emily but Carla, all he knew was that she was leaving, that they weren't getting along. That she couldn't stay clean. Maybe Emily didn't want to speak ill of her sister by saying she found drugs or get her in trouble with the law but still...

"No. That's not the whole truth."

"So, you're calling Emily a liar?" Kyle said.

"No. I mean. Sure. Yeah, she found drugs but I wasn't using them. I bought some because I fell off the wagon but I never took them. And I apologized to her."

"Get out of the truck," Travis said, repeating what Kyle had told her.

"Seriously? You're going to believe him over me? A guy who smacked Emily?"

Travis looked at Kyle. He'd had eyes on him most of the time. "He has no reason to want his kids harmed."

"And I do? Screw you. Both of you." She reached for her bag and Travis took it before she could grab it so he could check what else was inside. Digging in, he found a revolver at the bottom. She hadn't told them she was taking one. "What's this?"

"I'm the owner. I'm allowed to carry."

He couldn't argue with that but it didn't bode well in light of the accusation.

"You think I sabotaged your brother's bike, is that it?"

"My brother has ridden motorcycles since we were teens. He might be absent-minded about other things in his life but not his bikes. And a brand-new bike? C'mon!"

"He forgot to gas up," she said. "Who's to say he didn't forget to fill the tank or tighten that nut?" She paused, studying them both. "You think I unscrewed the oil plug?"

"You were probing his bike," Kyle said. "You said you always wanted one."

"Bullshit. I was just admiring it so I didn't have to sit in the truck with you." She looked at Travis. "You can't honestly believe him?"

Travis had seen her crouched beside the bike. Her back turned to him.

"Why would I do this?"

"I don't know. Maybe to slow us down. Maybe Kyle's right. Did you fail to pay someone money for drugs? Is that what this is about? Because I've yet to hear about a ransom. Which to me means this is personal and if they can't get to you, maybe it was easier to get to those you love."

Carla looked frantic. "No. That's not it."

"Then what is it? Huh? Who's behind this, Carla?"

"Please. Travis. Get Emily on the phone. She'll vouch for me."

"But will he?" Kyle said with a nod of the head.

Travis followed his gaze toward the hospital, to the sight of Danny coming out, tearing off the paper identification code around his wrist. If he got wind that she was behind this, there was no telling what he would do. "Get out of the truck now."

"No."

Eyeing his brother, Travis came around and grabbed her by the arm, pulled her, and thrust her toward the rear. He slammed the door closed and told Kyle to get in.

"You can't do this. Travis."

"Go. Now. Before I tell him."

Carla looked off toward Danny who looked furious and in a lot of pain. He wouldn't be thinking straight and any accusation leveled would no doubt send him flying off the handle.

"Go! Now!" He took her bag, removed the gun, and tossed it at her. Carla snagged it up and turned and fled, disappearing into the night across the lot as Danny got closer.

Travis closed the other door on the other side. As Kyle passed him to go around to the passenger side, Travis grabbed him by the arm. "Don't say anything to him."

"I won't."

"And don't think this changes anything between you and me."

"You should speak with your brother." Kyle climbed into the truck as Danny approached.

"Where's Carla going?"

"She has things to take care of. Listen, Danny, what are you doing? You should be in there."

"I would be waiting until morning and even then, I'm not guaranteed to be seen. There are too many people, Travis."

"I can't take you with me."

Travis glanced at Kyle through the windshield.

"I'm fine. I banged up my elbow, that's all. I'll take some meds and..."

"You took one hell of a fall. Meds aren't going to help internal bleeding if you have it."

"I know my own body. I'm not waiting in there."

"Then I'll take you home."

"I can't do that."

"Why not?"

"Because I lost my house."

Silence stretched.

"What?"

"It's a long story. I don't want to get into it."

"But how?"

"I fell behind on payments. What do you think?"

"But you were doing fine."

"That's what you think."

Travis stared at him. "Why didn't you tell me, I could have..."

With his good arm, he reached into his jacket and pulled out a pack of smokes, and set one between his lips before lighting it with a Zippo. "Uh, I don't know, maybe because we haven't talked to each other in several years." He blew out smoke from the corner of his mouth.

Travis blew out his cheeks, releasing all the stress of the day. His gaze roamed the birds in the lot, the ones that hadn't been cleared away. It seemed like the world was falling apart around him and he was being asked in some strange way to deal with it, all at once. Emily, Anna, Danny, Kyle, and some kind of end-times extinction. "I tried, Danny. I tried but you hung up on me. You wouldn't answer the door. What do you expect me to do? I did everything I could that night."

"Everything?"

"I did what I thought was right. I followed protocol."

"If you had gone in there, maybe they would have been alive now."

"You don't know that. We don't know how things would have played out if I did it differently. And you can't expect me to take the blame for it either. I would have given my own life to see her and your kid here with you. And you know that. It was out of my hands."

"Was it?"

"You know damn well it was," he said, jabbing a finger at the ground and losing his cool. "And right now is not the time or place to discuss this. We've already wasted enough time. If you're coming, get inside, if not, go back to the hospital but I'm done explaining myself to you, Carla, or Kyle." Travis skirted around the hood and got inside, slamming the door. Danny stood there looking at him through the windshield. He blew out smoke, tossed his cigarette, and got in the rear of the cab.

Travis floored it out of there, wanting to put as much distance as he could between him and Vermont, the event, and the past. He only wished it was that easy.

15

She knew the odds of staying alive were low. Steph watched the two thugs talk quietly from across the room. Bound to the chair that was tucked beneath the dining table, she'd been wracking her brain. How could they get out of this situation? She glanced at the clock. It was late in the evening.

At some point, they would need to sleep.

She'd tried to break the zip ties but they were too tight.

There had to be a way to get the upper hand but she just couldn't think of it.

Lucas' face was red from tears. She was trying to remain strong for him but there was a good chance this wouldn't end well and they would end up buried in a shallow grave.

Rooster patted Bernard on the shoulder and he stepped outside for a cigarette.

"Look, if it's money you want. I can take you to an ATM but let the boy go, he's done nothing wrong."

Rooster pulled up a chair in front of her. "I've told you. All we want is a room for the night. Behave and nothing will happen to you or the kid. Screw us around and this could turn into a bad night for the both of you."

"What about sleep? We can't sleep here."

"I've slept in all manner of places."

"Please. We're not going to run. Where would we run to? These restraints are digging into our wrists. Can you just loosen them or take them off?"

Rooster smiled. "So you can overpower us?"

"I'm a hundred and thirty pounds wet, do you really think I'm a danger?"

He stared at her, a smile forming. "Don't play the I'm a woman card. Women are some of the most resourceful and capable people in this world. Now I go letting you out and you somehow figure out a way to screw us over, how would I explain that?"

"So, you'd have to explain it to someone. Who? Who put you up to this?"

"That's not important right now. Just stay relaxed and this will all be over soon."

"Well, that's the thing. I'm not relaxed and neither is Lucas. If you don't trust me, at least let that poor boy sleep in a bed tonight. I think you or Bernard can handle a child. Or are you incapable of even that?"

That hit a sore point. She'd thought about it since he'd made that comment regarding having to explain himself. It meant he wasn't the top dog, instead, he was one of the lapdogs doing the dirty work which meant he was lower down the ladder of hierarchy. Steph fed into that. Testing him to see if it got a reaction. One look at his nostrils flaring and she had him where she wanted him.

"I'm more than capable. More of a man than probably your dead husband."

"Then cut him loose and prove it."

"No, I'm not falling for your tricks."

She shrugged. "Fine. Only proves my point," she muttered under her breath. She said it loud enough that he heard. Rooster stared at her and then got up and went over to the kitchen counter and withdrew a large kitchen knife.

"Hold on. Look, I didn't mean anything by it."

"Yes, you did." He got closer in front of her and waved the tip of it inches away from her nose. Then, he moved around her and approached Lucas.

"Please. Please don't," she said.

He said nothing but had this menacing grin as he came behind Lucas. He took hold of his head with the palm of his hand and brought the knife up and around to his throat. "Now, you aren't going to be a problem, are you, boy? You see because if you are, not only will I hurt you, I will hurt her. Do you understand?"

He tried to nod but Rooster was holding his head hard.

"Good."

In one swift motion, he brought the knife behind and cut loose his restraints. "Don't let me regret this." He let out a whistle. Outside Bernard turned. He tossed his cigarette down and stepped inside.

"The boy will sleep on the couch tonight. Go get him a pillow and some blankets from one of the rooms."

"But Rooster—"

"Do it!"

He said it without taking his eyes off Steph. He wanted her to know he was in charge. That he wasn't someone's errand boy and he had the situation well under control. He then took his hands and placed them on Lucas' shoulders and held him there while he waited.

"You know, you'd be surprised who's in charge of this little shindig," he said. "I know you think I'm a bad person but you are wrong. In another life, I think you and I would get along well. Friends. Maybe lovers even."

Steph wanted to puke. She wanted to make her revulsion clear but right now that was one tool she had in her arsenal and he'd just reminded her. Men were a sucker for a woman, a woman who played up to the image they tried to project into the world. He wanted her to believe that he was in charge, at the helm of this operation, and more than capable, so she would feed into that.

"Perhaps," she said. She didn't want to lay it on too thick or he wouldn't believe that she was sincere. She wasn't but having a poker face was key right now. Just getting him to release Lucas revealed a lot about him. It meant that he had an ego, and regardless of his orders, he would place that above all else.

Bernard returned carrying an armful of bedding.

Rooster patted Lucas on the shoulders. "Time for bed, kid. Tomorrow you'll wake up and this will all be a memory. Nothing more than a bad dream."

Whatever this was, it was clear he didn't expect it to go beyond one night. Were they waiting on a ransom? Was that why they had taken Anna? Were they nothing more than pawns, insurance to make sure they got their money? She needed to know more. Anything that could help Travis. That required getting close.

After he returned from getting Lucas set up to sleep for the night, she asked, "Could you get me a drink?"

Rooster crossed the room and took out a glass to pour water in and she shook her head. "No, something stronger."

His lip curled. "A beer?"

"No, I was thinking some red wine. I have a twenty-year-old bottle over there that I have been meaning to open. I was going to keep it for a celebration but now I think it could come in handy to calm my nerves."

"You know, Steph... can I call you that?"

She nodded.

"You have nothing to worry about. As I said, I'm not the bad guy here. I'm not going to harm you or Lucas if you don't give us reason to." Her gaze followed him as he crossed the room, took out the bottle from a wine rack, and pulled out a few drawers searching for the corkscrew.

"The second one down," she said.

"I want this to go smoothly. I want to see you and Lucas safe and sound but that means you have to work with me." He skirted around the breakfast bar and stopped at the table in front of her with two glasses. He popped the cork and poured the lush red wine into her glass and set it in front of her. "Try to see this as one night, one night with good company."

"Good company?"

He nodded. "I'll admit we got off to a rocky start but that's to be expected to lay the ground rules. You can't get from A to Z without rules, without some direction. Now you know where we are heading and how you can get there, it's up to you if you want to get there or whether you want to veer off the road and find yourself trapped in a fireball. Make sense?"

She nodded, repeating back some of the key elements just so he knew she was listening. "Ground rules. Direction. One night. Good company."

"You got it."

"I'd toast to that but uh..."

"Ah. The predicament. Now I can't have you put me at a

disadvantage. But I get a sense you're listening. Are you, Steph?" He paused. "Listening?"

"To every word. I just want him to be safe."

"Good." He nodded. "And he will be. Just abide by the rules. Don't veer off," he said as he took the knife and cut her hands loose but not her ankles. He was testing her as much as she was testing him. A smart move. Like moving pawns on a chessboard, they were now locked in a game of wits.

Steph leaned forward and took her glass and sipped it.

"Good, isn't it," he said, leaning back in his seat and taking out a cigarette. "You smoke?"

"No."

"Ugh, probably for the best. I've been meaning to give up for years but just can't seem to kick it." He lit the end and blew the smoke away from her.

"So, your brother in Burlington, Vermont?"

"A story but you fell for it, right?"

She nodded.

"So, tell me, how much are you getting out of this?"

Rooster smiled and set his glass down. He leaned his arm against the table and crossed his legs. "Oh, we don't talk numbers. What's the point? You'll be fine tomorrow."

"Curious. I'm interested to know what kind of number made you agree to the risk."

He hemmed and hawed. "Let's just say it was large enough."

"And so, you're sure they're going to pay you?"

He laughed. "My brother and I always get paid."

"You've done this before?"

"How about we not talk about this? You know, you're a good-looking woman, Steph, it seems a pity that such a woman like yourself is going to waste."

"Waste?" She chuckled.

"Yeah. I mean, how long has it been since your husband passed?"

"Six years."

"Six years. And in that time, you've never dated?"

"Nope," she said, setting her empty glass in front of her. She tapped the top with her finger, gesturing for him to top her up. As someone that often drank wine, she was fairly good at staying sober while others slipped under the table. Her brother would joke that she had a hollow leg. He wasn't far wrong. Rooster leaned forward and poured more wine. When he was done, he glanced off into the living room where his brother was in a recliner beside the boy, with the TV on. A dim glow and hum emanated from the room.

"And why might that be?"

"Haven't found the right man, I guess."

"And what would this right man look like?"

"Why do you think that would be important to me?"

He laughed and took another drink. "Come now. Everyone is obsessed with the way a person looks. I mean, you don't strike me as a gold digger. Or... hold on. Was this your place before you met your husband?"

"It was his parents'."

"Okay, maybe you are."

She laughed, playing into his poor attempt at humor. "If I wanted money, I think I would have set the bar a little higher. Maybe a doctor, a lawyer, or some fancy CEO. Not a small inn in the back ass of nowhere."

"Ahhh... Not too keen on this place?"

"It's okay. I've always yearned for something bigger. Something I can sink my teeth into," she said seductively, though she was referring to a challenge. His gaze slipped down and she could tell the alcohol was beginning to lower his inhibitions. She wanted him to drop his guard, to overlook what she was doing. If she could just get him out of sight of Bernard, maybe, just maybe they could stand a chance of turning this around. "But, men like that are hard to find. They play too small; they don't take risks..."

"And you find that boring?"

"I find it..." she paused, searching for the right word, a word that might make him think about loosening his grip on her, "...restricting."

"No wonder you don't like those restraints."

"Oh, I don't mind them. Just not in this setting," she said, taking a gulp of her drink and letting that sexual innuendo hang out there in front of him. She could see a glint in his eye as if he was imagining it. Rooster looked over to his brother and Steph knew he was thinking about it, thinking about cutting her loose, taking her upstairs, out of sight, placing her in a vulnerable position, a position that could leave him vulnerable.

She decided to lay it on thick, close the window of what might be a good time to make him realize that he better decide before she passed out. "Wow, that wine is really hitting me. Makes me giddy, sleepy even. What about you?"

Rooster drummed his fingers on the table. She wondered if he was thinking about the level of danger. If he cut her loose, would she really be a problem? So far, he'd managed to control her. Keep her at bay. And that was before she had several glasses of wine. How much more now?

"You know, I think you and I should head on up."

"You aren't looking to take advantage of me, are you?" she said, chuckling giddily, allowing him to think the wine was taking hold. The reality was it was barely scratching the surface. Steph could polish off a whole bottle by herself before she felt the real effects.

"Do you want me to?" He grinned back at her.

Oh, it was there. The banter, the fake connection, the draw. He was no longer thinking with his brain but was leading with what was between his legs. She yawned and looked toward Bernard who was eyeing his brother. He was larger. Much larger. Even if she could overpower Rooster, Bernard would be a challenge and he was close to Lucas.

What are you doing? she asked herself.

One wrong move and she could find herself with a bullet in her.

One mistake and she wouldn't get another opportunity. This was a one-and-done situation. One chance to turn the tables and level the playing field. She took a deep breath and smiled back.

"Lead the way!"

16

In a blinding rage, Bill threw Anna onto the bed. He wasn't sure who angered him more — Pam for nearly losing her or Anna for causing trouble. After the night he'd had scouring the town for insulin, this was a slap in the face. "You ever do that again, and it will be the last time." He paced within the cramped confines of the RV. "I just spent the last hour searching for insulin to help you and this is how you repay me?"

Through tears, she snapped back at him without fear. "You don't want to help; you just don't want me dead. I'm no use to you dead."

"Listen to me, little girl. You are my ticket out of this shit-hole into a better life and nothing, and I mean nothing is going to stand in the way of that. Not you. Not your mother. Not your pops. No one. So, you better show me some damn respect or I will personally put you in the grave and I'll do it while you're alive."

Her eyes widened and he knew he had her terrified. That was where he wanted her to be, so scared of what might happen that she wouldn't even think about running again. It was his mistake. He should have established that right from the get-go.

Bill turned to leave.

"Did you get it?" she asked.

"No."

"Then maybe you will end up burying me," she said. He looked back at her as she curled into a ball like a wounded animal and began to cry hard. He hadn't considered this. Had he stuck to the plan, Emily would be dead and they would be rewarded, but he'd had to hedge his bets, cover his ass. For there was no telling how this would end. At least this way, it should be a sure thing.

He closed the accordion door and made a phone call.

Bernard picked up. "Yeah."

"Where's your brother?"

"Busy?"

"Get him on the phone."

He heard him place the cell close to his chest and call out to Rooster. While he was waiting, he looked out the window and saw a couple walking toward the RV. Marcus approached them and from what he could tell got into a little bit of an argument.

Had they heard her?

Seen her?

Shit. That was all they needed. He'd planned to head out on the road several hours ago, but the need to get insulin had thrown a wrench in the works. Eyeing the confrontation, he knew Marcus and Pam could handle it.

Rooster got on the line.

"Glad to see you checking in on time."

"Is the boy secure?"

"Of course. And you? What is that noise?"

Rooster could hear the arguing in the background, which had now made its way to the RV.

"It's nothing. Look, you need to make that call. We are moving up the timeline."

"But that isn't meant to happen until the morning."

"Well, things change. Look, I've gotta go. Handle it."

He hung up, took out his Glock from the back of his pants, checked the ammo before placing it back, and then headed out. "Do we have a problem here?" he asked, making it clear that he wasn't about to have anyone walk up to his RV without a good reason. At this stage there was no point in trying to avoid conflict, it would happen one way or another. Now or later.

The couple were middle-aged. The guy looked as if he was stitched into a shirt, he was large, six-foot-tall, with a thick heavy beard, and lots of heavy rings on his fingers. He almost looked like a biker with tattoos down his arms, and a T-shirt that said Ride Hard. The woman, a full-size beauty, carried herself with as much confidence as he did.

"A girl. We saw a young girl screaming."

He thumbed over his shoulder at the RV. "Oh, that's my daughter. She's acting out. She's autistic."

"Oh," they said in unison. "It's just that it looked a little odd."

"It can be that way. Bright lights. Loud noises. Stress. Anything can set her off, isn't that right, darlin'?" Bill covered up the gun in the back of his jeans with his shirt, no longer feeling as though they were a threat. "You'll have to forgive us but with everything that is happening in the country right now, the birds and whatnot, she's a little concerned."

"We understand. How is it out there?" the large, bearded fella asked.

"Bad. Really bad. The roads are clogged. People are looting."

"Sounds like folks are anticipating that it will affect the economy tomorrow. Man, they don't waste time, do they?"

"The early bird gets the worm," Bill said. He put an arm around Pam and tried to act as if they were one big happy family, one big misunderstood family. "Well, it's late. We'll be turning in for the night."

"Right, yeah, we should do that too," the guy said to his partner who wasn't buying it. The bitch was standing there with her arms crossed, all high and mighty, glancing at the windows of the RV trying to spot the girl. Bill glanced back hoping that little brat wasn't there, trying to signal them. He wouldn't think twice about killing these two people. He'd drop them where they stood. He didn't want to do it but if it came to it, he would take out anyone that stood between him and his future.

"Where are you all from?" the woman asked in a manner that almost made her sound like a cop.

"Here," he said. "New York."

"What city?"

"Albany."

"So, what brings you up to this RV park?"

"A little R&R," he said with a smile, gripping Pam's shoulder. "City life can mess with you, you know? We like to come here. It's peaceful."

"So you've been here before?"

"Oh yeah."

That was the mistake he made. But it wasn't his, it was theirs.

"Strange. I haven't seen you around here before. Have we, Mike?" she said, glancing at her husband. The bearded fellow looked at her, then them. "You see, we own this lot," she remarked. "We see the same people return here and are always aware of new folks."

Pam was quick to offer a reason.

"He means the area. Not the park."

Bill had to hand it to her. For all her screwups, she did come in handy.

"Oh, right," the woman said. "My mistake." She smiled politely and tapped her husband. "Well, you folks have a good evening." They turned and walked away and Bill didn't take his eyes off them.

Even as Marcus turned to go back to the RV and Pam made a comment about how they needed to get moving, he watched the couple. The woman turned and looked back and said something to her husband.

He didn't buy it for one minute that they had bought their story.

And even though the emergency lines were still tied up, people like that could be a problem. They'd seen their faces. They had their RV details. If they woke up tomorrow and the world had managed to reel in disorder, would they squeal to the pigs? Damn, right they would.

Squeezing Pam's shoulder hard, he turned her and escorted her back to the RV.

"Bill, you're hurting me," she said. He nodded, pursing his lips as Marcus opened the door and he led her inside. As soon as they were out of sight he tossed her against the couch and then backhanded her.

"You dumb bitch. I will deal with you later. Marcus. Let's go."

"Where?"

"You know where."

"But they bought it."

"Like hell they did."

He wasn't going to allow them the chance to screw up. Before he opened the RV door, he looked at Pam. "Make sure she doesn't escape this time."

They headed into the inky night, making their way over to the owner's office, slipping past multiple RVs. They didn't take a direct path toward the door just in case the woman was looking out for them. Instead, they skirted around the perimeter of the lot. He reached around and pulled the Glock, then glanced at Marcus, who had a shotgun in hand. There was no sneaking up, no waiting for their moment. No, there was no need for that. No need to worry about what others would think. Under the cover of darkness, it would all be over fast.

Bill burst through the door, gun raised. The guy was already trying to get through to emergency services. He caught the drift of it as they entered. "911 isn't answering, maybe..."

Crack. One round, he fired into the guy, then another, as he was still walking forward. The woman screamed; all her hard exterior melted at death's door. Marcus introduced her to the reaper with two pumps of the shotgun in her back.

Bill loomed over the man who was coughing blood out of his mouth.

"That's right. That's right. No help is coming."

The man's eyes flared as Bill leveled the gun at him and squeezed the trigger.

They didn't linger. Marcus snatched up the woman's handbag off the counter and a pack of smokes and they exited as coolly as they had entered. Though now they made a beeline for the wooded area, working their way around at the sound of people coming out of RVs. They wouldn't hear their screams, or the cries for someone to call 911, because as soon as they made it back to their RV, Marcus hopped into the driver's seat, and Bill got in the truck, and they peeled out into the night, ready to begin the next leg of the journey, toward wealth, toward freedom.

17

She didn't want to kill him but she would protect Lucas with her life.

Steph gave her best performance of having had too much to drink. She slipped on the steps on the way up and her shoe came off, tumbling down. She giggled and fell back against Rooster. "Whoa, steady there."

"Wow, that wine was strong. But you are far stronger." She laughed. "I knew there was a reason I was holding off drinking it."

"Bernard. Keep an eye on the boy."

Bernard leaned against the doorway to the living room with his arms folded. "Rooster. We agreed."

"Just do it," he said, waving him off.

What Rooster hadn't seen her do was snag up the corkscrew when he answered the phone call. Whether it was a simple mistake, or a lack of judgment from drinking too much, he never said a word. The implement with its small wooden handle and extended twisted metal was now down inside her bra. The steel was sticking into her breast, causing a fair amount of pain, but it wouldn't compare to what he would feel when she stuck it in his jugular.

It would have to be that.

Something quick.

That would ultimately disable him from chasing her down, from calling out to Bernard. She staggered up two flights of steps, now and again feeling his hand on her ass as he felt her assets. She wanted to swat him off but he had to buy it. He had to believe she was too inebriated to care and that she was nothing more than a poor helpless widow who was eager to jump into the sack with the first asshole who came along. "You know, Mr. Rooster…"

"It's just Rooster."

She let out a noise that made her sound like one. It made him laugh.

It was all part of the performance. Keep it light. Fun. Giddy.

"You were saying?" he asked as they continued down a small hallway toward her bedroom with an ensuite bathroom.

"What was I about to say?" She shook her head. "Oh, that's right. Have you ever been married?"

"Nope."

"Come on now, a man like you? A take-action, take-control type of guy? I would have imagined they would be lining up," she said, giggling as she turned and ran a hand over his face and down his chest. He pressed her up against the wall before they even made it to the room and held her wrist, studying her, as if looking for the flaw.

"What are you playing at?"

"Playing?"

"You know. This. Us."

"It was you who suggested it."

"Yeah but..."

"Well, that's what comes from getting a woman drunk," she said, turning away from him only to have him grab her and press her up against the wall again, and mush his tobacco-tasting tongue into hers. She would have killed him right there and then if she could have reached that corkscrew but instead, she allowed herself to sink into it. When he broke apart, he gave a wry smile, took her hand, pulled her into the room forcefully, and used his heel to kick the door closed. Without wasting a second, he lifted and tossed her onto the bed and began to unbutton his shirt.

"I need to freshen up," she said, going to roll off the bed but he grabbed her and pressed her down, crawling on top and straddling her as he undid his shirt.

"No, you're fresh enough."

"I need to use the bathroom," she said again.

He took hold of her shirt and tore it open; the buttons flew in every direction.

Then he stared hard at her body. For a second, she thought he could see the corkscrew but the room was too dark and it was hidden beneath her breast.

"You are spectacular."

He brought a finger down to slide off one of the bra straps but as he did it, she stopped him. "Wait."

She reached for his belt buckle and began undoing it and instinctively he rolled off, thinking she was going to service him. Oh, he was about to get serviced, but not in the way he imagined. Sliding over the top of him, she brought her lips down to his chest and let them brush against his skin. She felt his back arch at the slightest touch.

As she gently clawed at his skin with one hand, she

reached into her bra with the other and extracted the corkscrew that was no bigger than four and a half inches. It fit snugly in her grip as she continued to touch his body with her lips.

She felt his hand press against her head, trying to guide her down, but she wasn't going down, she only had one location in mind. Laying her left arm across his wrists, as if she was wanting him to hold her there, she brought the corkscrew up slowly and lifted her eyes. His head was back in some ecstatic pose as if he was riding the waves of bliss. He was delusional to think that she would ever give herself to a man like him, too full of ego to accept that she could ever pull the wool over his eyes.

But she did.

It all ended fast, as she swung the corkscrew around and jammed it into the side of his neck with as much strength as she could summon.

He gasped but not a single word came out.

He was struggling to capture one breath, though his hands clamped onto her hair tightly as if trying to inflict pain on her, but it was pointless. A swift turn and he released his grip.

Steph moved up the bed, over him, bringing her lips to his ear.

"Thanks for the good company."

She extracted the corkscrew with one pull and sat up to watch him bleed out.

18

All these vehicles and not one had a charger? Emily had searched six abandoned cars and she still hadn't found a charger that could fit the iPhone. Two looked hopeful but she couldn't get inside because of their mangled state.

Out of breath, in agony, she dropped beside a vehicle, phone in one hand, tire iron in the other, as a text from Anna came in. Three short words sent her into a panic.

On the move.

She went into the Find My Device app and noticed they were heading northwest.

Did they say where they are going?

Seconds passed before another message came back.

No idea.

Have you heard their names?

Yes, the guy in charge is called Bill, the younger one is Marcus and the woman is Pam.

Finally, she had something to give Travis. Something that might allow them to connect the dots. Now they knew how many they were dealing with, that they were in an RV, and had a black truck. If they could get through to the cops. Maybe they could help.

Oh, who was she kidding? One look around and it was clear that help was far from at hand. *Listen to me, darlin', how much of a charge do you have left in the watch?*

Forty-three percent.

I have far less in this phone. If I don't respond it's because I've run out of power. I'm trying to find somewhere to charge this. Just know that Travis and your father are on the way. Okay. They will find you.

She needed to know. There was no guarantee the phone was going to last and Emily wouldn't let her feel abandoned.

I'm so scared mom.

Have they hurt you?

Not yet.

It was reassuring but now they were on the move, going where? Was the RV park just one stop along the way? Were they trafficking her and if so, would they be taking her to a buyer? Emily told Anna she would be in contact again but needed to find a charger. She sent a quick text to Travis to let him know that they were on the move heading northwest. She got up; excruciating jolts of pain went through her right leg. It had ballooned and was throbbing so hard. Mentally the only way she could stop herself from crying was to keep her thoughts on Anna.

Hopping on one foot, she made it over to another vehicle and peered inside. It was so dark that she had to turn on the flashlight on the phone but that used even more power.

Inside she saw a white cable dangling.

A quick try of the door and she found it was locked.

Drawing back the tire iron to smash the window, she felt a

hand grab her wrist.

"What the..."

"Trying to break into my car, are you?" a rail-thin woman said.

"Sorry. I thought it was abandoned."

"And that gives you the right to smash the window?"

The woman looked like a meth head. Wiry graying hair was pulled back behind her head, and she wore loose-fitting clothing. "I'm sorry. I'll leave."

"You're not going anywhere. Police. Help! This woman is trying to break into my vehicle," she bellowed loudly while holding Emily's wrist. She was a lunatic. There were no police out here. Was this even her car?

"Let me go." Emily struggled to break the woman's grasp but she held tight, now grabbing her clothes.

"Police. Anyone!"

"I'm leaving," Emily said.

"The hell you are!"

Emily did the only thing she could. With her other arm, she balled up her hand and fired off a left hook, dropping the woman like a sack of potatoes. Staggering away on one leg and dragging the other behind, she looked back to see the woman using her vehicle to climb to her feet. "You bitch. You're going to pay for that."

A shot of fear went through her. She wasn't made for this.

She'd always been one to back down from confrontation. If it was a war of words. Fine. She could deal with that but going head-to-head, throwing fists. That had always been Kyle's department.

In the hours that had passed since the accident, most of the people who had crashed or were unable to get through the graveyard of steel had abandoned their vehicles and hiked to the nearest town. Those with working vehicles had turned around and gotten on the hard shoulder.

There were few willing to wait by their vehicles in the cold and dark of night.

With the steady sound of car alarms that hadn't stopped since the accident, her cries fell on deaf ears. Besides, pleas for help had been the chorus on the highway, one more did nothing. "Someone. Help. This woman's..."

Before she got the words out, she felt the woman run up behind her and shove her full force to the ground. Anna's phone flew out of her hand, hitting the asphalt and sliding under a car. But that was the least of her troubles.

Like a tiger, the insane woman pounced on Emily's back and grabbed clumps of her hair, and smashed her forehead into the ground. Her survival instincts kicked in. Fight or flight. Emily brought back her elbow, driving it into the woman's ribs twice before she fell off her. Rolling, Emily latched onto the hag and punched her twice in the face.

All the while her leg felt like it was on fire.

Clawing away, desperate to escape, she felt a meaty hand grab her bad leg and pull. She might as well have taken an axe to it. Broken, fractured, whatever it was, it was already in excruciating pain. Now it felt like she ramped up the pain too unbearable. Still holding the tire iron, she lashed out and struck the woman in the head. It should have knocked her out, it didn't. That crazy woman just kept coming at her, determined to beat her to death.

Emily used her good foot to kick her in the face before using the front of a beat-up Honda to clamber to her feet. She looked at the woman who was no longer moving and sighed. All that and she'd done nothing to the woman's car.

With tears rolling down her cheeks, she staggered over to

the car where her phone had gone under, hoping to collect it. Just as she dropped to a crouch beside the vehicle, she heard the woman let out a howl. The hag was up again. There was no stopping her. She just kept coming. She was on her feet and barreling toward her. Emily's eyes flared.

She didn't have time to attack her with the tire iron. The hag slammed into Emily so hard with a knee that her head bounced off the car.

That's when everything went dark.

SECONDS, minutes, hours, it was hard to know how much time passed. When Emily came to, her head felt like someone had hit her with a sledgehammer. She was lying beside the same car. The woman was having a cigarette, staring at a phone. Her spine was pressed against the car, her knees were drawn up, and she was swiping the screen of the phone.

With blood trickling into her eye, Emily groaned.

The woman looked at her. "I'll take this," she said, showing her the phone. Anna's phone.

"No. I need it," she muttered, barely able to get the words out.

The woman stood up. "You're lucky I didn't kill you." She began to walk away.

Although her vision blurred, she could see the tire iron nearby. Pulling her body over to it, Emily clamped onto it and drew strength she didn't even know she had to rise to her feet. The woman had walked a good eight feet away when she noticed.

"You don't give up, do you?"

"Give me the phone," Emily said, wiggling her fingers.

"You want this?" She showed it to her again. "Go get it!"

The woman tossed it as far as she could over the tops of the cars into the ditch.

"NO!"

Laughter erupted from the woman as she turned to walk away.

After everything that had happened, Emily lost it and threw the tire iron at the woman as hard as she could. It struck her in the back of the head and she collapsed to the ground, her skull bouncing off the asphalt. Emily stood there for a second waiting for her to get up but she didn't. Staggering over, she looked down and saw blood spreading outward from her head. Shock set in hard and fast. Dropping to her knees, she shook her. "Hey. Hey, lady. Wake up. Get up."

But she didn't. She wouldn't.

Fear overwhelmed her.

She'd never harmed anyone, let alone killed anyone.

Emily looked around, had anyone seen her do it? This couldn't be happening. She placed a hand on the woman's neck and noticed there was no pulse. Tears rolled down her cheeks as she got up and backed away, moving toward the ditch.

Looking out into the dark, into the thick grass, she knew she didn't stand a chance in hell of finding the phone. Still, she tried. Eyes roaming, feeling her way through the sea of green.

Nothing.

There was no illumination coming from the phone. Right there and then, Emily dropped to her knees, feeling the weight of the world hit her.

How long she remained there was unknown.

It was a call that came into the phone from Travis that helped her find it.

She hadn't been far from it — a few feet at the most when the screen lit up and it jangled. Tears of relief and stress mixed as she answered it.

Emily answered his call, but she was a complete mess. She could barely form words, let alone a sentence. "Hey, hey, slow it down. Emily, relax, take a breath." He repeated this multiple times until he could make sense of what she was saying.

"You did what?"

"She came at me. I..." Emily trailed off.

Travis veered over to the edge of the road and killed the engine.

"What are you doing?" Kyle asked. He didn't answer him. He got out to have some privacy and walked a short distance behind the truck.

"Take me through that again."

She repeated herself. He didn't know what to say. His officer mindset kicked in. Had she killed the woman while they were fighting, maybe that could be deemed self-defense, but throwing a tire iron? "Look, there is nothing you can do about it now. Take the phone, and put some distance between yourself and the victim."

"I'm so sorry. Travis. I'm so sorry..." she said as if it was him she needed to apologize to. It was her that would have to live with it. Under the circumstances, it seemed that anything could happen. She wasn't the only one to witness the insanity of the mysterious event. Fights had broken out along the highways as some people tried to get rides from those with working vehicles, while others tried to steal gasoline. He'd been listening to the radio on the way out of Vermont. Looting had started in many of the major cities and there were reports of a few shootings.

"Listen to me. What is done is done. You can't change that." He figured he would shift it back to Anna. "Have you heard from her? Any update?"

"She's on the move. Hold on, I'll get you directions." She accessed the app and looked at the last update. A moment later she said, "They've gone north. By the looks of it, they are heading into Fort Edward."

"All right."

"Travis, she has some names." She reeled them off.

"Are any of those familiar to you?" he asked.

"No. Could you ask Kyle?"

"Yeah, sure." He skirted around the truck and ran them by him.

Kyle shrugged. "No idea."

"He doesn't know," Travis said, getting back on the phone again. He walked to the back of the truck and leaned against it, knowing he was going to have to tell her about Carla.

"God, Travis. I can't believe it's come to this."

"Listen..." he was about to tell her but then decided not to. One more bad thing could send her over the edge and he already felt as if she was teetering. "Take a breather. We'll get this all worked out. Just stay on that phone."

"It's running out of charge."

"How much left?"

"Less than 20 percent."

"Shoot. Can't you find a car with a charger in it?"

"That's what I was doing when it happened. Look, I have

to go," she said. "I need to find something before..." The line crackled and he wasn't sure if she hung up or it dropped due to a loss of signal.

"Emily? Emily?"

He dialed back but got no answer. "Shit!" He slammed a fist against the truck panel and it made a soft indentation sound then slapped back into place. He stuck the phone in his pocket and got back in.

"Everything okay?" Kyle asked.

"No, Kyle. Nothing is okay," he said, starting the engine and sticking the gear in drive. He glanced over his shoulder to check on his brother. "You good?"

"I'm just dandy."

At least that was one thing he didn't have to think about. So far, Danny had been showing signs that the accident had just badly bruised him and broken his arm. Although it needed to be treated, Danny didn't want to hold them up but he also didn't want to be left behind. Veering out onto the road, they continued on their way, heading north now that they were in the state of New York.

The journey would take them through a lot of rural areas. The next real town would be Cambridge, before that was nothing but the countryside, trees, and fields for miles.

"You've never heard of a Bill, Marcus, or Pam?" Travis asked.

"Never," Kyle replied. "By the way, earlier you said Emily was using Apple and tracking. How's that work?"

Not everyone was an Apple user.

"Her watch. iPhone has an app that lets you Find Your devices. You can also use Share My Location which lets parents see where their kids are at."

"Huh. And you say they're now on the move."

"Yep."

"Look, no offense, Danny, but maybe we should drop you off at a hospital," he said, looking at his phone. Travis glanced over his shoulder.

"What do you say, brother?"

He narrowed his eyes. "No. Keep going. We don't have time."

They continued in silence. About five minutes outside of Cambridge, Kyle turned on the radio and scanned the channels for news on the event as well as local traffic. They'd run into a few blockades that required going a different route. Fortunately, out in the backcountry, there weren't as many vehicles on the road when the birds fell, so there were fewer accidents. Along the way, they saw people thumbing for a ride but they never stopped. It was too dangerous. With everything they'd seen so far, they couldn't take the risk of someone trying to steal the truck.

"Look, we're going to need to stop before Cambridge," Kyle said.

"Why?"

"Nature calls."

"Go in the woods."

"I need to take a shit."

"Danny, in the back with my gear you should find some toilet paper."

"You are joking, right?" Kyle said.

"No. There are times when I'm miles from a town. Where do you think game wardens go? I always come prepared."

"Yeah, well that's the difference between you and me. Us municipal cops use a thing called bathrooms. C'mon, I'll be in and out. It's not like we are going to get there any faster. What's a few minutes longer?"

19

Steph remained on top of Rooster until the light in his eyes faded. As soon as he was gone, she climbed off, slipped into a new shirt, removed her shoes so Bernard wouldn't hear any noise, and then collected Rooster's gun.

The grip felt too large in her small hands.

Too heavy for her to wield accurately.

Besides, she'd never fired one in her life. But how hard could it be? Point and shoot, right?

Fishing through his jacket pockets, she came across his phone. She tapped it. There was no lock on it. She was about to see who he'd been speaking to on the phone when Bernard shouted up the stairs.

"Rooster!"

A cold shot of fear went through her.

If he didn't answer, Bernard might come up.

Frozen, clutching the gun, Steph didn't dare move.

She figured he'd clue in that the two of them were having sex but he didn't.

"Rooster. Bill wants to know why you never called."

Bill? The name didn't ring a bell.

"Come on, Rooster."

She heard heavy footsteps coming up the hardwood staircase. "Damn it, Rooster, you've always gotta make things difficult."

Think.

Think fast.

Steph moved across the room and closed the door. There was no lock. She could wait for him to enter and shoot him but if she missed — she could be the one chewing a bullet. She hurried back to the bed and flipped the covers over Rooster's corpse. She removed his boots and socks and then made it look like he was face down.

All she needed was a moment of distraction.

Seeing them together might be enough.

But there was so much blood. The mattress was soaked as were the covers. She had another cover bundled up in the closet, a thick winter duvet. Quickly snagging it up, she threw it on top of the bloody one, crossed the room, dimmed the lights some more, and then climbed into bed beneath him.

Her heartbeat was pounding fast. Her hand clutching the revolver.

Half of her body was beneath Rooster with one arm free so she could take the shot from beneath the covers if need be. She could hear Bernard approaching, walking down the hallway toward the bedroom.

She could feel blood soaking into her clothes, making her back stick to the bed.

Steph stared up at the gray lifeless face of Rooster and wrapped a hand over his head, pressing it against the one side of her neck as if he was biting it. She began to thrust her hips ever so slightly to make it look like he was in motion.

Moaning, she eyed the door, expecting any second for him to enter.

And he did. The door cracked open and he peered in but under the dim lighting, the only thing he would be able to see was their silhouette and maybe her face. She opened her mouth wide and continued to thrust her hips giving the illusion that they were going at it.

"Rooster," he said in a low voice, holding a phone in hand.

Her finger twitched against the trigger under the covers. If he got closer, she would squeeze. At this range, the chances of her hitting him were slim to none. She couldn't afford any errors. Eyeing Bernard from across the room, she offered him a winning smile, as if she was enjoying it. That was enough for him.

"He'll be right there," she said with a wink, continuing to thrust her hips. All Bernard would have seen was the wave of the duvet, and his brother's feet peeking out, moving ever so slightly. Bernard paused, and for a second, she thought she was made.

Then he backed out of the room, and she heard him on the phone.

"He's busy, Bill."

As soon as Steph heard the sound of his boots on the steps, she shoved Rooster off her, and bounced out of the bed, and padded over to the door. Peeking out she could see he was gone. With the blood rushing in her ears, Steph moved out of the room onto the landing and made her way to the top of the stairs. Every step felt like she was about to stand on a land mine. She winced, hoping it wasn't an area that would creak and give her away.

Downstairs, she could hear the low drone of the TV and Bernard talking on the phone. There could be no errors. One wrong move and it would be over for Lucas, and her. Living in the house, she had become acutely aware of which steps on the staircase creaked more than others. Placing her back to the wall, she stepped over two of the steps and worked her way down.

"I've already told him that," Bernard said.

"I need a drink," she heard Lucas say.

"Look, Bill, I have to go. I'll get him to call you."

She worked her way back up the steps as he'd have to walk by to get to the kitchen.

No sooner had she reached the top and gotten behind the wall than she saw him come out of the living room and enter the kitchen. The faucet turned on. There was a flush of water and then he returned with a glass.

Back down she went, moving faster this time.

Every step made her think it would be her last, that he would hear her and come barreling around the corner. But he never did. Steph reached the last step and peered around the corner into the dimly lit living room. The TV flickered; its light made shadows on the walls. She looked in and could see Lucas but not him. There was a sunroom off the main living room. He could have gone in there to have a smoke, but why bother? He could smoke inside.

Something wasn't right.

Lucas was sitting far too still. Almost like a doll or as if he'd been instructed to stay still because...

Steph went to step into the room when a hand shot out from around the corner, grabbing her by the throat and throwing her back. The gun went off then flew out of her hand, landing somewhere in the darkness. She hit the hardwood floor and slid across it, slamming into the closest wall.

Pain shot through her shoulder, radiating through her body. She looked at him, hoping the round had hit him, but if it had he wasn't showing any sign of pain.

"You must think I'm stupid," he said, taking out his handgun from his jacket to kill her. Lucas burst into view, smashing him in the shin with the fire poker. His leg buckled and he let out a howl.

Lucas followed through with another to his back but it was like hitting him with a twig. He yelled and struck back, knocking Lucas against the wall.

Steph scrambled to her feet to try and get Bernard's revolver that he'd dropped.

Lucas returned with as much resilience as an adult. He jumped on Bernard's back, trying to put the poker around his neck, but a boy of his size looked like a fly on his shoulder. Bernard swatted him and then reached over his shoulder and tried to shake Lucas off, but he kept moving and dodging his hand. That was the thing about bodybuilders, their ability to reach the middle of their back was more challenging than for someone with less build. "You little bastard!"

Steph made a mad dash for the gun only to be winded by a front kick to the gut.

Eventually, Bernard managed to latch on to Lucas and he tossed him across the room. He landed hard, slamming into the wall and going unconscious.

Steph screamed wildly at the sight. She snatched up the fire poker and drove it hard into Bernard as he bent down to scoop up his gun.

The tip of it went in his shoulder and although he almost

managed to grab the gun, she forced him back into the room and the two of them toppled over the back of the sofa, landing hard on the coffee table.

The sheer weight broke the table.

Coughing hard, she tried to get her bearings before he did, but she was too late. Bernard, furious and bleeding, rose above her, yanked out the poker from his shoulder, and lifted it high, bringing it down with bone-breaking power.

The first strike missed because she rolled, she wasn't as fortunate with the second. It smashed into her hip, producing a scream from her lips. It was beyond any pain she'd felt before. The next one was even worse, hitting her shoulder and tearing her shirt.

Crack.

A gunshot echoed loudly.

Followed by another, then a third and fourth.

Bernard dropped the poker, his mouth widening.

Both of his legs buckled and he fell face forward, landing beside Steph.

With her heart drumming hard, Steph's eyes went from Bernard to Lucas who was holding the gun with both hands.

She would have been beaten to death if he hadn't done that. There was no doubt in her mind. "It's all right. Lucas. You can let it go. He can't harm us now," she said, struggling to rise, pain coursing through her with every move. Lucas' hands were shaking, his knuckles white from where he was holding the gun so tight. He couldn't peel his eyes away from their attacker even as Steph reached him and loosened his grip on the weapon.

Stepping back from the mess, she wrapped her arms around Lucas. His body was trembling hard. The boy leaned into her. No tears were shed but he was traumatized nonetheless. "I'm sorry. I'm sorry."

"No. You don't have anything to be sorry about," she said, sinking to his level. "Thank you," she said. "Come on." She took him out, away from the macabre scene. She led him into the kitchen and set him down on one of the stools around the kitchen island then got out a glass and some pop, and set it down in front of him along with a bag of chips, anything to take his mind off what had happened.

She scooped up her landline and tried to call the police but just got a busy signal. Setting the landline down, she told Lucas to wait there while she went and retrieved Rooster's phone. She'd left it in the bedroom.

Upstairs, she entered and collected the phone without looking at him.

She would have to drag Rooster and Bernard out back or leave them until police arrived. But that wasn't what was on her mind right then. She tapped his phone and looked at the contacts. Among the list was Bill's name and many other phone numbers, one of which was familiar. There were multiple calls.

"Why?" she muttered. Her mind quickly connected the dots.

She phoned and waited for the person to pick up. A few rings and they did.

The male voice answered, "I told you not to phone me."

She had to know how they would respond.

Steph hung up immediately, shaking her head.

MILES AWAY, Emily was fighting her own battle.

Emily stared at her phone which was almost in the red at less than 6 percent. She couldn't move fast enough, going from car to car trying to find a charger. Most were locked, others that were open had nothing.

When she finally found a car unlocked with a cable dangling from the charger, there was no key in the ignition so it wouldn't start, which in turn meant no power. She attached the phone, hoping on a wing and a prayer that it would miraculously charge the battery, but it didn't register. "Damn it!" She pounded her fist against the dashboard so hard that it made her hand hurt.

Crying, she refused to give up.

Emily got out but this time didn't get far before she collapsed. The pain in her leg was bad enough before the woman yanked it but now it was overwhelming her. It was crippling.

In the distance, she could see the dead woman.

This was punishment, some form of karma. So many thoughts went through her mind. She wanted to scream at the world. How? Why her daughter?

There on the ground, she lifted the phone and tapped out one last text that she sent to Anna and Travis.

Power is almost gone.

Anna replied almost immediately, fear in her words.

Don't leave me, mom.

I'm still here, she replied.

Emily began to cry even harder.

She sent another text to Travis, telling him to text from here on out. Even though there was only one number for both the phone and watch, at least once the phone died, Travis could still message Anna. But he wouldn't be able to track her. That required...

Her thoughts wandered back to the days before Anna's birthday when she went shopping for the watch. She'd specifically wanted to get something that would allow her to know where she was. Fear. Being mindful. Some might have said it was controlling but if anything happened to her, she would get the blame for not having done her due diligence in providing a way to track her. What did you say? she muttered, thinking of what the rep had said.

"Yes, you can share an Apple ID or agree to share location or you wouldn't need her phone or yours and could use the iCloud website."

That was it! But that relied on knowing her email and password.

Her stomach sank.

What's her Apple login? she thought. *Ask her what her login is.*

Emily texted her again. The message was delivered. *Yes.*

Under the pressure of the situation, it hadn't even registered to ask that. She was so overwhelmed and just glad to be able to communicate with Anna and certain that she would find a charger that she didn't think to ask.

Now she had.

She waited for an answer.

Her eyes darted back and forth between the red and iMessage.

C'mon, c'mon, Anna.

If a response was delivered, she didn't see it because the screen went black. She was out of power, and out of time.

20

It was a dingy restroom nestled in the forest.

Kyle's need to stop had taken them off the main stretch of highway snaking north and had them cutting through Mount Tom State Park, which was sandwiched between Shaftsbury, Vermont, and Cambridge, New York. In and out, that's what he'd told him. He didn't want to linger any longer than a few minutes.

While Kyle and Danny disappeared around the corner and entered to relieve themselves, he waited in the truck, swiping his phone and checking messages. He'd been driving when Emily's message about low power came in. By the time he was able to respond, it seemed as if it was too late.

He tapped out a reply but got nothing.

Minutes passed. Travis glanced up but they still hadn't come out.

He honked the horn then checked his messages. This wasn't boding well. Without her guidance, Anna was lost. There was no way they would be able to find her. Travis honked his horn again. "Goodness sakes!" he said.

Right then his phone rang. It was Steph.

"Hey, how's it going?"

"Is he there with you?" she asked.

"What?"

"Listen to me..."

"Steph, what's the matter?"

She brought him up to speed on what had happened: the attack in the parking lot, Rooster, his brother, and her killing them. Hearing her reel it off seemed surreal. He knew his sister; she wasn't one for exaggerating, neither would she dump this on him, knowing the circumstances they were facing.

But it was when she dropped Kyle's name that his stomach twisted.

"His number was in this guy's phone. There were multiple calls made to him. Days, weeks before this, and several a day before today. He knows him. And if he knows Rooster, he must know Anna's captors."

"Are you sure?"

"I called the number."

Travis lifted his eyes toward the restroom. They still hadn't emerged. As Steph continued to tell him about what she'd found out, the situation with Danny's bike now made sense. If he was involved in some way in kidnapping Anna, what was he hoping to gain? It was his daughter. "Look, I gotta go," Travis said.

"Travis."

"Steph, I've..."

"Be careful."

He hung up and turned off the engine. He got out of the truck and withdrew his service pistol. Travis made his way up to the restroom and walked around the side which was out of view. He stood in front of two doors. One was for women, the other for men. He slowly eased open the door on the men's, hoping it wouldn't make a noise. It opened and he stepped inside expecting to see them washing their hands, but no one was at the faucets though the hand dryer was on.

Travis glanced down the line of three stalls. He dropped down and could see Danny's boots but they weren't moving. The other stalls were empty. Almost instantly Travis turned around at the sound of something metallic sliding into place. He rushed toward the door and yanked on it but it wouldn't budge.

"Kyle! Kyle. Open this door!"

On the other side, he heard him. "It wasn't meant to go down like this."

"Why would you do this to them?"

"I didn't. They did."

"What the hell are you talking about? Why did you do this?"

"Oh, Travis. You said it yourself, there are only three reasons besides money why someone abducts a child: to traffic, to kill, or to raise them. And I'll be damned if I let anyone else raise my child. I should have dealt with her myself. Now I will."

With that said he walked away.

"Kyle. Kyle." Travis pulled hard on the door but it wouldn't shift. "Come back. Don't do this. Don't you do it!" He shook the handle violently but it wouldn't budge. Whatever he had inserted into the handle, it was holding fast. Travis hurried back into the bathroom and kicked the door open on the stall his brother was in.

He found him, his head leaned against the sidewall, a knife in his stomach. "No. No." Travis dropped down and looked at it. Danny was still alive but barely holding on. "Don't you die on me!"

He turned and looked around, taking stock of the situation. High above, the window, if it could even be called that, was thick squares of opaque glass. Far too thick to smash, purposely made that way to deter vandalism. Anger rose inside at the sound of the truck roaring to life. He'd taken the keys with him so Kyle must have hot-wired it.

Travis cursed loudly, returning to his brother.

Crouched in front of him, he placed a hand on the side of his face. "Stay with me, brother."

"I'm sorry, Travis. I'm sorry for blaming you."

"It's okay. It doesn't matter."

"I should have told you sooner. I've wasted so many years." He coughed hard and winced.

"Just hang in there."

Frantic to do something, anything, Travis took out his service weapon and fired several rounds at the glass but it did little except cause large hairline fractures and drill a few holes. It was thick blocks.

"Why. Why!" he said, wracking his brain.

He crossed to the door and tried again, this time placing one foot on the wall and the other behind him and then pulling with all his strength. He gritted his teeth and tried again. No luck. It was too secure. Travis slammed a fist against the door, his frustration boiling over. He went back inside and climbed up onto the washbasins to try and peer out but it was too thick.

"Travis."

He glanced over his shoulder. His brother's skin had gone pale.

Dropping to the floor, Travis entered the stall, he took

hold of his brother and dragged him out, setting him down between his legs so he could lean him back against his body. "I can hear them," Danny said.

"What?"

"Shailene and Eric. They're calling me."

Several tears trickled out of Travis' eyes and rolled down his cheeks. All Danny had wanted since losing his wife and kid was to see them again. Maybe now he would. Still, it shouldn't have happened like this. Not this way.

He'd carried so much grief over the last few years, a sense that he should have done more, that he had let his brother down at a time when he was relying on him. That moment came back like a flash.

Danny was out of town on business when Travis got the call to attend a domestic in progress in a rural setting, about half an hour outside of Eden Falls. He was the nearest warden on duty at the time and until a state trooper could get there, he responded. When he heard the address from dispatch, his stomach sank.

It was Danny's home.

Not knowing that his brother was out of town, he'd expected to find him there. He'd expected to find out that he'd had a few too many to drink, that he'd gotten into a heated exchange with Shailene. He figured he'd be able to talk him down, have him stay over at his house and they'd have things patched up in no time.

What he didn't know was that a local meth head had forced his way inside and was now holding Shailene and their eight-year-old son Eric hostage. Somehow Shailene had managed to call the cops.

Because of yelling in the background, and Shailene whispering, the dispatch was unable to understand entirely what she was saying. They couldn't determine the threat level or the real truth.

He only found out how dangerous the situation was when he rolled up outside their property. The lights in the house weren't on. He had no sense of the situation turning into a problem because it was his brother's house. He'd visited countless times. Shailene and Danny got into it once or twice a year but that was it. Danny cared too much to stay angry. That just wasn't his way.

Like it was yesterday, he found himself back there.

Stepping out of the truck, taking off his ball cap, and tossing it in the truck.

He saw their family car outside, so again, he didn't think for a minute that Danny wasn't there. What he found out later was Shailene had dropped him off at the airport and then returned.

Travis strolled up the short driveway, hand on his service weapon, thinking of what he was going to say to his brother when the glass shattered and shots were fired at him.

One round had struck him in the upper right shoulder, spinning him and sending him down. Travis had scrambled back, getting in touch with dispatch and alerting them to the situation. As he was conversing with them, he saw the door open and someone come outside holding Shailene from behind, gun pressed against her rib cage.

"You better get out of here!" the gaunt fellow bellowed.

With the radio mic in hand that controlled the speaker on the roof, he glanced through the windshield at the guy. "Listen to me, I'm a game warden. How about you let the woman and the kid go and we can talk about what you want."

"I want you gone. That's what I want."

"All right. But you know this place is going to be swarming

with cops in about thirty minutes. Put down the gun and let's talk. Surely there is something you want."

"Everything I want is here. With my wife, and my boy!"

His wife? His boy? The guy was delusional.

"My name's Travis Young. I didn't get your name," he yelled from behind his truck.

"Get the fuck out of here or I'll kill everyone including myself!" he shouted then dragged Shailene back into the house and slammed the door. Situations like this could go from zero to sixty in seconds. One wrong move, one wrong word and it was over.

It was clear this guy was as high as a kite and under some impression that this was his home and worse — Shailene was his wife now living with someone else. Travis had been called out to enough domestics where an ex-husband had shown up and given his ex-wife a beating because she'd moved on. Those situations never ended well and that was with guys who weren't even on anything. But this guy. He was loaded. He was a stranger. He didn't know Shailene. He had all the makings of a tweaker. A meth head. His skin was blotchy and deteriorating. Rotten teeth. Twitching like mad, eyes bored into his head from a lack of sleep, food, and water. Lines down his arms from multiple needles going in.

Getting back in touch with dispatch, Travis was put through to one of the deputies on the way out, this time bringing SWAT. He knew that the odds of Shailene staying alive before they arrived were low, but if the tweaker saw SWAT, there was a good chance he would end it right then.

After he relayed the situation, the sergeant on duty had told Travis to stand down. Do nothing. They would be there in twenty minutes and handle it from that point. He had agreed and tried to keep the guy calm by getting back in the truck and pulling out, but as he was doing that, Danny had phoned, saying he was unable to get through to Shailene and wanted to know if there was a problem.

A part of him wanted to lie. But he couldn't. He told him straight out what had happened. Immediately he went into panic mode. "You have to get in there and do something. You know as well as I do, he will kill her as soon as he sees the cops. Get in there, Travis. Find a way in. Kill that bastard. Don't you dare let them die!"

He was putting a lot on him, especially in a situation that was out of his control, where there was protocol to follow. But this was his brother. And he knew better than anyone the odds when a meth head was in charge. Travis couldn't tell him he would go in. Instead, he told him everything was going to be fine. He'd regretted those words.

After hanging up, he'd contemplated going in. Maybe it would have worked out if he had. Instead, he hung back and did what was expected. He didn't break protocol. He didn't charge in guns blazing, like some whacked-out hero from a movie. No, he waited for backup, for SWAT, for those who were trained for this exact situation.

Everything will be okay; he'd told himself that even as he heard screams from the house and more yelling. He tried to talk to the guy, get him to calm down, but it was like trying to reel in a rabid dog. He didn't listen to reason, and he sure as hell wasn't going to be told what to do. No, the gun came out of the window several times and he fired rounds the moment Travis got too close.

When Travis saw the black SWAT van rolling up, and multiple cruisers, he was strangely relieved. Now it wasn't all on his shoulders. He was telling the lead cop what the current situation was and that he'd only seen one armed suspect when three shots rang out.

He could still hear the echo as if it was yesterday.

Immediately after, SWAT stormed the house, and found Shailene and Eric dead. The meth-head had taken his own life.

Snapping out of the past, Travis noticed Danny wasn't moving or breathing.

He held him tight, his eyes welling up as anger rose inside. God, if he'd just dropped him off, stopped him from going with them. He'd still be alive.

Right then, he heard the door unlock.

Travis grabbed his gun, ready to unload if it was Kyle returning to finish him off. It wasn't. "Travis?"

Carla came around the corner and her eyes widened.

"Carla."

"It was him, wasn't it?" she said, gritting her teeth.

"How did you find us?"

"I followed from a distance in a vehicle. I saw you all head into the state park. I waited outside, but when I saw your truck go by without you all in it, I figured I would come and see what happened."

She gazed down at Danny.

"Did Kyle do that?"

Travis nodded as he got up. "I'm sorry. About what happened back at the hospital. I know it wasn't you. I just..."

"Bought into his lies. Yeah, he has a way of convincing people. It doesn't help that he's a cop," she said. "I on the other hand knew it was that bastard. But for the life of me, I couldn't figure out why but then it all fell into place. You here. Me gone. He didn't want any of us to make it to Anna or Emily."

"Because of the custody battle."

She nodded. "She had a slam-dunk case against him. And he knew it. The only way he could end up with the kids was to make sure she was out of the picture."

"But she's still alive," he said. As the words came out, it dawned on him what Kyle meant when he said *I should have dealt with her myself. Now I will.* Kyle wasn't heading to get Anna. He wasn't worried about her. "He wants Emily dead. Shit! Listen, help me get Danny into the car."

Carla took hold of his brother's boots and he lifted him underneath his arms and they carried him out, over to a Nissan Rogue. She opened the back and they slipped him inside. "Look, if we go into the next town and find another vehicle, I'll head to where Emily is and you head for Anna," Carla said.

He nodded then groaned. "No, no, NO, I can't."

"Why not?"

"I don't know where she is."

"But Emily's tracking her, right?"

"She was. The phone died and they're on the move."

"Shit," Carla said, bringing a hand up to her face. "And I can't even phone her to warn her that he's coming. Damn it!"

Carla paced, thinking of what to do. "We could both go. Once we get there, we could charge the phone and then..."

"No. It will take too long. I need to get to Anna before she..." His heart sank as he ran both hands over the top of his head. "Shit. No. No!"

"What is it?"

"Anna's insulin was in the truck. Damn it!"

Carla opened the driver's side and reached in. "You mean this?" She showed him the insulin pack.

"What the hell, how did you...?"

"There was no way in hell I was going to leave it with him. After that happened? But still, without knowing where she is, it's not going to be of much use."

Travis thought for a minute. "Hold on a second." He phoned Steph and she picked up.

"Travis, you okay?'

"Danny's dead," he said just coming straight out with it. "Kyle killed him."

"Sonofabitch."

"Look, is Lucas there? I need to talk to him."

"Yeah, yeah."

He heard her call for him. While he was waiting, he brought Steph up to speed on what happened, and how Danny died. She began crying then sniffed hard and blew her nose. A moment later Lucas got on the phone.

"Hi."

"Hey, Lucas. You probably don't know but I thought I would ask. You wouldn't by any chance know Anna's Apple login and password, would you?"

"Um. I think so. You might have to try a couple of passwords as I'm not sure if she changed it but I used it because I didn't have a phone, so I would take hers from time to time. It really annoys her." He chuckled.

"Lucas, you are a lifesaver."

Travis reached into his pocket and took out a pen and his notepad and had him reel off the information. Once he had it down, he thanked him and let him go. Immediately after, he brought up the website for iCloud and tried the email and then two passwords. The first didn't work, the second let him in.

Inside, there were several icons before him. He clicked on Find iPhone.

Not only would this tell him exactly where Emily was on a map, even though the phone had no power as it would show the last place the iPhone was before the battery died, but there was an option under All Devices for Anna's Apple Watch.

He clicked on it and breathed a sigh of relief.

There it was. The small green dot. Still on the move.

He did the same for the iPhone and then turned it and showed Carla. "Let's get moving," he said. This time he wasn't waiting for permission to handle the matter, everything relied on him, and he wouldn't fail.

21

Kyle was both elated and confused.

Free now of the weight of Travis, Danny, and Carla, he could finish what he'd set out to do in the beginning.

However, Anna being abducted wasn't part of the plan. When he was a good distance outside of Mount Tom State Forest, barreling south toward Albany, toward the woman that had caused him so much agony and embarrassment, he phoned Rooster. He'd called earlier but for some reason, Rooster had hung up.

This time he got an answer, it just wasn't the one he expected.

"Rooster?"

"He's unavailable," a familiar voice replied.

"Steph?"

"You bastard. Did you really think you could kill Emily, and Anna, and Lucas?"

"I don't know what you're talking about."

"Enough with the games. I know what you did. But it didn't work. He's dead."

"Who's dead?"

"Who do you think!?"

Rooster. No, it was impossible. He was with Bill. He wasn't meant to be in Vermont. That was... he trailed off. His thoughts started making connections.

Bill had been an informer for the Bennington Police for over four years. Originally, he was a crack dealer working out of the county. When state police busted him sitting on a large number of amphetamines, they saw gold. Because of his connections in the drug world, they had worked out a plea deal that would keep him out of prison in exchange for information. They felt he was worth more as an informant than on the inside. Bill, a coward who only showed a false bravado around those that followed him, jumped at the chance.

The arrangement was he'd move among the underbelly of Vermont and help them work their way up the chain to the top brass, the kingpins that were importing into the state. It had worked. They'd turned over more drugs in the last few years with his help than ever before. It had even helped Kyle climb the ladder to several awards.

Everything in his life was on track until his marriage fell apart.

It hadn't started badly. There was a time when he thought the world of Emily and would have done anything to make her smile, but daily rubbing shoulders with the underworld had taken its toll on him. It had stripped away all that was good and made him cynical. He'd seen more shit than he cared to mention. It wasn't long before he began self-medicating. When he wasn't taking small packets of coke from evidence to snort, he was numbing out with a six-pack of beer every night. The world just became a blur and with it, his wife and two children. From that moment on, he was on a direct course to becoming shipwrecked. He was surprised it didn't happen sooner.

It was around that time he'd gotten into it with Emily. A blazing fight, slamming doors, screaming at one another, and then in a split second, he'd lifted a clenched hand to her face.

That gesture alone had sealed his fate.

He saw the look in her eyes. The fear. The emptiness. The repulsion. He'd become like the men he'd arrested. Unhinged. Out of control. And too far gone to dial it back without ruining everything he'd achieved. He knew it was over but was too proud, too egotistical to walk away or let her just slide out the door and ride off into a better life. No, she was his, his wife, his family, his property, no different than Bill was his two-bit informant. There to serve his purpose.

He got high on people doing what he said.

Maybe that was what pushed him over the edge.

Emily just wouldn't do what he said.

Still, even in the worst moments, he thought he was safe, untouchable.

He figured Emily was too scared to rat on him, he thought he could control her the way he had the lowlifes on the street through threats and intimidation. But she was above that and saw him for what he was, a washed-up cop who had traded honor for disgrace, and honesty for lies.

Not in a million years did he think she would try to destroy his reputation in the community, with the department, or friends.

And the kids... trying to get the court to give her full custody? That was a joke.

Over his dead body.

That's what he'd thought at first. After chewing it over with a drinking buddy, the thought came to him of another way to handle it. Dispose of her and his problems would go away. The court would have no other choice than to give his kids back to him. That's when his mind began churning. But how? He drank late into the evening thinking of how he could pull it off. He couldn't be connected to it. There also had to be a reason if someone did connect the dots as to why she was killed. Bill would be the scapegoat, nothing more.

The rumor mill had already been spinning for years that Bill might turn the tables on the cops and take them out so he could free himself from the burden of being an informant. No one believed it. But it was known he'd given it thought. That's when Kyle approached him and delivered a proposition, one he couldn't refuse. He would pay Bill to kill his wife and make it look like an accident. A car accident, a bump from behind on a busy highway, veering off into a tree, a railing, a ditch, over the edge of a bridge — he didn't care how it was done so long as it was done right, clean, and couldn't be traced back to him. In exchange, he would pay Bill a hefty amount, money that was lifted from evidence, evidence that wouldn't make it into the locker or any logbook. And to top it off, he would pull a few strings and make sure he was released from his duty as an informant.

Of course, that's what he told him and he would follow through if it worked.

If he was problematic, he would pin the whole damn thing on him. He already had a recording of Bill threatening to harm his family. A nudge in the right direction and Bill would be on his way to county lockup.

He had this.

It was foolproof.

But at no point in any of his exchanges with Bill was taking Anna part of the plan. Had it gone wrong? He didn't know Anna was with Emily that day, hell, he didn't know Lucas was with Travis. That was because of the temporary custody order.

Snatching up his phone, he made the call to Bill.

He answered, all full of himself. "Deputy Mansfield. What can I do for you?"

"It's not what you can do, it's what you've done. I told you very clearly that my kids were not to be touched, taken, or in any way around when you killed her. Which incidentally... you didn't do!"

"What are you talking about?"

"She's alive. My wife is alive, you idiot."

"She was upside down, unconscious in an SUV that was on fire."

"Oh, she was very much conscious, you moron. Now you want to tell me why you have my daughter? And she better be alive."

"Relax. Don't you worry! She's alive. For now." He paused. "It's simple really. It's called insurance. Did you really think for one moment I bought that whole spiel about payment and release?"

"Huh?"

"You see, deputy, for four years you have been using me, throwing me one lie after the other. Now the tables are turned. How does that feel?"

"You mother fu..."

"You want your kids back. This is how it's going to happen. You will deliver the money you promised and I will hand over Anna to you. Then, you will pull those strings you promised and get in writing my release as an informant.

Once I have that and it's verified, you will have your boy back."

"Lucas?"

"You got it."

Kyle pulled off to the side of the road. "Oh, I underestimated you."

"We all make mistakes, deputy."

Without missing a beat, Kyle shot back, "Like the one you made sending Rooster to Vermont?"

"Huh. How did you know that?"

"The same way I found out my wife was alive. Through others that KNOW ABOUT IT!" he bellowed down the phone. "I can't believe I trusted you to pull this off. You're a fucking idiot."

"Watch it. One phone call and your kid is dead."

"Really? And how do you suppose that will happen when the guy you sent to do it is dead and so is his brother?"

"What?" he stuttered.

"That's right, moron. The men you sent to watch over my boy and that woman are dead. She killed them. So, listen very carefully. Unless you want to end up in prison for killing my wife and my daughter, you will do exactly as I say."

"Your wife? But you just said she's alive."

"She is. Soon, she won't be. I'm going to clean up your sloppy work. When I'm done, you and I are going to have an exchange. Money for Anna."

"And the release?"

"You'll get your release but only once I have her."

"But that's not the deal."

"No, it wasn't. Neither was me having to go and do the job you were meant to do. So, I think we have a deal. Agreed?"

There was a pause.

"Agreed."

"Now, tell me what the condition of my daughter is, and get her on the phone."

"Well, that's going to be a problem."

"GET HER ON THE PHONE, BILL!" he bellowed.

Bill snapped back. "No can do. She's in a different vehicle from me."

"She's diabetic."

"I know."

"If anything happens to her, you can kiss the money goodbye... oh, and that release you want... you'll get it at the end of a bullet."

"Then you better get that money to me soon."

"Where are you now?"

Bill reeled off a random location.

Kyle told him to wait while he located an area on the map that would work. "Head south toward Albany. Let's meet in Round Lake at the boat launch."

Kyle hung up and tossed the phone on the seat, anger getting the better of him.

He sat there for a moment thinking about how he would pull this off. Time was ticking. Not only did he have to handle Emily, but he also didn't have the money on him. He wasn't even aware that Bill had set the wheels in motion. He was meant to call him. Let him know when it was done and then he would get the cash. He veered back on the road and weaved his way around a wreck, gripping the wheel tight, his mind now shifting to Emily.

He knew Travis wouldn't be able to alert her now that her phone was dead so it would just be him and her out on that highway. By now those who were alive would have hiked out to the nearest town. He knew what highway she was on. Not the exact spot but how many broken-legged women could there be? It's not like she would have hitched a ride or walked out. She'd spent too much time focusing on Anna.

He felt a twinge in his gut.

This was becoming all too real. This was the reason he'd hired Bill.

He didn't want to kill her but now he had to.

He thought this would keep his hands clean, that in some weird way he'd be able to set his head down at night knowing that he hadn't touched the mother of his children, someone else had. And for that crime, he'd be punished. It was meant to be a win-win situation. Emily gone. Bill in jail. Good reigning over evil.

And it still could be.

Hell, he might even elicit the sympathy of the community.

22

The alarm bells were ringing. She was going to die.

If she didn't get insulin fast, her body would begin to break down fat and muscle and it would lead to DKA — diabetic ketoacidosis. The bloodstream would become so acidic that she would develop dangerously high levels of ketones that would make her dehydrated and soon lead to organ failure and all manner of nastiness.

Anna flushed the toilet in the RV and returned to her bed. With her body so tired, they no longer bothered with restraints. Although she'd lied about the timing of her last insulin injection, in the hope they would take her to a hospital, she didn't even have to check her blood sugar to know that her body was screaming for insulin.

It was called the 4 Ts. They were the symptoms that she and others would notice — a need to use the toilet to urinate more often, being extremely thirsty and yet unable to quench that thirst, a feeling of overwhelming tiredness, and looking thinner from losing weight. It wouldn't be long before her vision would blur and her body would shut down. It varied from person to person, hours, days. No one could put an exact stamp on how quickly a person would respond.

"You don't look good," Pam said, checking in on her.

Her vision was beginning to blur, all she wanted to do was lie down and sleep but if there was a chance she could escape, that was far more important. Pam stood there staring at her before she closed the door once she saw her reach for water. The silly woman thought that water alone could prevent her from going into a coma. It was good but it wasn't an insulin replacement.

Gulping down a large amount of water, she thought about what the other side was like. The world had so many views, so many opinions. Depending on the culture a person was raised in, the religion or lack of one, a person could be stepping into the best place ever or the worst.

Would these people that had taken her be harmed in the next life for their actions in this one? Or would there be grace for them? She shook her head. Her mother hadn't raised her to believe in God but her grandmother had tried. Not in a forceful way or in a way that would scare her as she'd said what good was faith if it was embraced out of fear? But her grandmother wanted her to know that there were things that went beyond human understanding, and perhaps that was the area in which faith dwelled.

Balling up into a fetal position, holding on to a pillow, Anna thought about her mother. Never seeing her again, never hearing her voice. She couldn't imagine it. She didn't want to. She thought about Lucas, and the times she'd ignored him when he wanted to go to the park. She thought about her friends, and strangely even Travis.

Right as she was having that thought her watch vibrated. Mom? She glanced down to see an iMessage from Travis.

Hey kiddo, Travis here. I'm coming for you. I can see where you are. Your aunt Carla will go get your mother.

But mom has my phone, she replied.

I have access to your iCloud, she shot back.

How?

Lucas gave us your Apple login.

A smile formed. Like most little brothers, Lucas had been a thorn in her side at times. If he wasn't taking food she'd bought, he was often using her cell phone. Peering over her shoulder, he'd seen her tap in the password to her Apple account when she went to buy an album. He'd wanted it so he could download games. They'd gotten into a big argument and she'd told herself she was going to change it but hadn't gotten around to it. Now she was even more grateful for him.

Travis, they haven't given me insulin, my body is starting to go haywire.

There was no response.

Travis?

I hear you. I've got fast-acting insulin with me. I'm not far now. Do you recall the color of the RV you're in?

She thought back to when she'd broken out of the RV and had looked back.

It's white, the lower half is cream-colored. She whispered into the phone. The door to the bedroom opened and Anna stuck her wrist underneath her.

"Who are you talking to?" Pam asked.

"What?" she said, looking up at her through tired eyes.

"I heard you talking."

"Oh. That. It's a part of the process. Without insulin my body begins shutting down; you can start hallucinating. I thought my mother was here."

"Huh." Without any sense of care, she shut the door and Anna quickly checked the last message Travis sent.

I'm on my way. Hang in there, kid.

On the way to where? They were moving. If they didn't stop soon, he would be playing a game of cat and mouse all over the state, and with so many miles between them, he wouldn't stand a chance of catching up. Anna knew she needed to do something. Anything to get them to slow down — to narrow the distance between them and Travis, wherever he was. Using the one thing they were convinced about, her diabetes, she opted for that. "I'm going to throw up. Pam. I'm going to throw up!" she said multiple times.

Pam slid the door open.

"Well get in the toilet, girl!"

Anna hurried for the bathroom but stopped short.

"I'm not going to make it. This is going to be..." She began gagging, putting on her best performance. She'd mastered it pretty well, even used it in the past to get a day off school. Her familiarity with how her body responded when she really did throw up was pretty good. And with so much water in her stomach from having drunk four big glasses, she could quite easily bring up her stomach contents with two fingers down the back of her throat. It didn't take much.

Using that as a means to send the message to her, she bent over fast, with her hair covering her face, so Pam didn't see her stick her first finger into her mouth. A gush of water burst out all over Pam's boots along with foul-smelling bile.

Pam let out a scream as if she'd seen a rat. "Are you kidding me! Marcus! Marcus! Stop the vehicle." Again, Anna did it, flooding the carpeted floor with small chunks of what she'd eaten earlier that day. The look of repulsion on Pam's face was priceless. "Oh, the smell. Marcus, would you stop the damn vehicle. I need air. I need to..." He veered off and slammed the brakes on. Within seconds, Pam was out that door.

Marcus turned around and grimaced. "Oh, God."

He got out of his seat and hurried to the sink and pulled out a bucket from beneath it. He tossed it at her, not wanting to get close. He pulled his sweater up over the lower half of his mouth and followed Pam out.

Anna stifled a laugh. Of course, it wouldn't be long before she wasn't laughing and her body was nauseated and she really was throwing up but right now, just seeing those morons' reaction was a welcome change.

HAD they stopped or found her watch?

Travis kept his eyes on the road as he rode shotgun alongside Carla on the way through Cambridge. He tapped out a quick message to Anna to confirm. The response from her was almost instant.

I'm buying you some time.

Clever kid. Smart like her mother.

He set the phone down and kept his eyes peeled on the road. After the incident in the state forest, he'd needed to obtain a vehicle as Carla would take this one, so she could head for Emily.

Despite all the vehicles on the road that had crashed and drivers who had abandoned theirs, none that they came across had keys in the ignition. Instead, they'd opted to drive into Cambridge, New York, a short distance away, and stop at the local police department. He figured it would allow him to kill two birds with one stone — one, he could potentially obtain a working vehicle, and two, if there was a way for them to alert state patrol, they might be able to reach Anna and Emily sooner.

Of course, he was a realist. The chances of finding them alive were low, and only getting lower by the minute. But it would give him a chance to assess the situation that had sent the country into a spin.

"Just wait here," he said to Carla before heading into the stretched-out grey government building with black steel roofing that contained the police department, municipal offices, and courtroom. Outside there was a tall white flag-pole flying the American flag and nearby was one police cruiser.

Inside, behind the counter, an officer was collecting some gear in a bag when he looked up through the hardened glass that divided the front foyer from the office. "If you're here to file a report, you'll have to wait. We are a little overwhelmed right now."

"I'm not here for that," he said.

The cop was wearing glasses. He squinted as he made his way over.

"Vermont? What are you doing this far up here?" he asked.

"Dealing with an abduction," he said. "My daughter." Although that wasn't exactly true, God willing, Emily would become his fiancée and Anna his stepdaughter.

"You got an ID of the suspect?"

"Names. That's all. There are six of them involved. Two tried to take out my son in Vermont. Look, I know where she is, at least I do right now but I have no way of getting there."

"How did you get here?"

"A ride. My sister-in-law."

"Why can't she take you?"

"She's heading to Albany. You see, my gal's ex is..." He hated to say it because he knew cops stuck together through thick and thin no matter what, and without evidence or information that could verify his story, it would just be his word. "A cop from Vermont. They're going through a divorce. I believe he's going to harm her. Look, is there a way you can alert Albany or state?"

He chuckled. "Hell, we are a shithole in the middle of nowhere and are overwhelmed, can you imagine what it's like in the cities or elsewhere? Since the cattle started dying, people are losing their minds."

"Cattle?"

That was new.

"Yeah, you haven't heard?"

He shook his head.

"Whatever this is, it's not just affecting the birds and fish. Farms in the area have been reporting a large number of cattle found dead. Seems like this thing, whatever it is, biological, or a disease, it's moving fast and has now reached farm stock."

"But that's..."

"Going to affect everyone. Fish. Yeah, we might be able to manage without that, but cattle, now things have gone to the next level."

"I've seen looters."

"Yeah, I wouldn't be surprised if it doesn't start here soon. Once everyone gets news of the cattle dying, panic will set in, we've already seen it here with people buying everything in the store. So, look, friend, I'd like to help but... I just dropped back in to get some more supplies. With a lack of EMTs out there, we're having to help those who are stuck in vehicles."

"I understand." He nodded. "Sorry to have bothered you."

It was worth a shot. He couldn't expect an officer under these conditions to lend him his cruiser. It was too much to ask. But, as Travis went to walk out, the cop said, "Hey, hold up..." Travis looked back. "Give me the information on your lady friend and daughter. I'll see what I can do. I can't promise anything."

Travis reeled off the details of what he knew about the location of Anna. He even showed him the last location for Emily.

"And... what's your name again?"

"Travis Young. I serve out of Bennington County."

The cop nodded as he brought out his phone and looked up Fish & Game in Vermont. He glanced at his uniform and jotted down his badge number. Having received the 2019 Warden of the Year award, not only was his name and phone number on the Vermont Fish & Wildlife website among the other game wardens, but an article and a photo of him receiving his award were on there as well.

The cop looked at him. "Exceptional performance. Outstanding casework with a 100 percent conviction rate. You should come and work for us." He grinned. "I'm probably going to regret this but here." He reached into his pocket and took out a set of keys. "Around back you'll find my truck. A black Nissan Titan. You scratch it, you fix it, and I want it back... or... Travis Young, I will come and find you. You got it?" He winked and tossed the keys to him. "Just make sure it's fully gassed up when you return it."

He didn't have to offer it. Most wouldn't have but many cops took home their cruisers so it wasn't like he would be without a ride.

And after seeing the way Kyle had been, it restored his

faith in law enforcement. Not everyone was an asshole and most genuinely wanted to help even when they couldn't. "Thank you."

"Ah, I figure if I don't give it to you, you'll probably carjack someone. And right now, we're dealing with enough. Besides, it's one less report to file," he said with a laugh, turning away. Travis headed out, with a deep sense of gratitude. He glanced at his phone, watching the green dot that hadn't moved since he last looked. Whatever Anna was doing, it was working and that small window of time would give him a chance to catch up.

As soon as he was out, he jiggled the keys in the air, so Carla could see. She drove up around the back and made sure the vehicle was working before she left. The engine roared to life and he backed out, sidling up beside her. She brought her window down.

"Be careful, Carla," he said.

"You too. Oh, and don't forget this," she said, reaching over to the seat and then tossing him the insulin cold pack.

There was a sense as they looked at each other that maybe this was the last time they would see each other. The odds were stacked, the stakes high, and the clock ticking down on the lives of Emily and Anna.

He only hoped they made it there in time.

23

Emily tightened the blanket around her shoulders. Her injured leg was outstretched behind her as she dragged it over to a Toyota Camry. After losing power on the phone, she'd frantically tried to find someone with a phone she could use if only to call Travis, but a lack of people nearby and the pain of her swollen leg had all but made her give up.

With darkness wrapped around her and few if any people on the highway, she'd resolved to deal with her injury the best way she could — finding painkillers, water, food, and shelter for what she imagined would be a long night.

Three cars later, she found a bottle of travel Tylenol. She'd knocked back four with the dregs of coffee that had been sitting in a car for long enough that a small amount of gunk and green mold had formed on the surface.

Now with a passenger seat reclined, she struggled to sleep.

She clicked on a flashlight found in the trunk. *On. Off. On. Off.*

The cycle lit up the car ahead and cut into the night.

Several cars had passed by, and she'd tried to thumb a ride, hoping to get into the nearest town and to a police department, but that had only garnered stares from people in vehicles as they rolled by. No one was stopping for her. Or for anyone.

Something had changed. It wasn't just the birds she'd seen fall or the fish she'd read about on the phone. Something had taken hold of the people, filling them with so much fear and panic they just wanted to get home. She couldn't blame people for not stopping to help. The entire highway earlier that day had been filled with accidents, and injured victims. The need was too great. And where would they have taken them? By now hospitals had to be turning people away or lining them up outside on the ground.

The few people she saw looked in shock.

Some were unresponsive, others deadly. She considered the woman she'd killed. She'd never killed anyone in her life. She couldn't even reason it away as self-defense as the woman was walking away when she threw the tire iron. Sure, the hag had attacked first but did that justify what came next?

She no longer cared.

All she cared about was making sure her daughter was safe.

The noise of an engine, another vehicle approaching pulled her out of her thoughts.

Over the past hour she'd tried to alert vehicles to her presence by turning on and off the flashlight, hoping that if someone rolled by, they would see it. Ultimately, she was praying emergency services would spot her, but they never came, and the response was the same every time — vehicles just kept rolling by.

This time, however, a vehicle stopped.

She lifted her head and peered out into the darkness.

Clicking the flashlight off so her eyes could adjust, she noticed it was a truck.

Black.

The red taillights blinked on, indicating it was backing up.

That's when she recognized the emblem on the door. It was unmistakable.

It was Travis. Huge relief flooded her chest as she reached for the handle to get out. As she swung her feet out, confusion kicked in, the sixth sense that something wasn't right. The kind of wary gut reaction that brought questions to mind. He couldn't have made it here unless he abandoned Anna. Had he left her behind? Had something gone wrong and he was without insulin? No.

Stumbling out into the darkness, she squinted as the driver's door opened and the cab lit up, illuminating the occupant. She didn't need to see his face, as soon as Emily saw the uniform, she knew who it was.

Her heart began to drum harder. Her breath getting louder in her ears.

Had they decided to separate? She didn't know. As much as she hated Kyle, seeing him was a relief. "Kyle!" she yelled. Standing on the truck's running board, he peered over the top of the cab.

"Over here!" Emily staggered to her feet, placing a hand against the Toyota to support her. Kyle switched off the engine but left his driver's door wide. He skirted around the back end of the truck and slipped between the front end of the Toyota and a Hyundai's back end. The two vehicles had collided.

She stumbled forward. "Thank God you came. I was beginning to think I would be out here all night." She looked past him and then back at him. "Where's Travis, Carla, or his brother?"

"They went on to get Anna. I said I would swing down and get you."

She nodded, a frown forming. "Oh, okay."

"He said you had a busted leg, that right?"

"Yeah, yeah, but it's fine. Just help me get in the truck."

"No, let me take a look at it."

She stared at him and whether it was the uniform or that she knew him, she nodded and dropped down on her butt and extended her bad leg. Kyle dropped to a knee, clicked on his heavy Maglite, and let the light wash over the wound as he hiked up the pant leg. "Geesh. That doesn't look good."

"Yeah, it's a bad break. But at least it didn't break the skin."

He nodded, looking up at her, shining the light in her eyes. She squinted and brought a hand up to her face as he scooted up and examined the rest of her to check for other injuries. "I'm a little banged up, and have a few cuts but nothing as bad as that leg."

"Yeah, that's good."

"Any word on Anna?" she asked.

"Hmm?" he replied, looking distracted as his gaze roamed around as if he was looking for someone to help.

"Anna. Did she try to contact you?"

"Uh. No. But Travis knows where she is."

"How?"

"What?"

Again, distracted. He was fidgety. Acting odd, like he was unsure of himself.

"How would he know? I tried to get her password for the iCloud but—"

"Yeah, he got it."

"But I never gave it to him. She never even gave it to me."

"She told me. Yeah, a while back."

She knew that wasn't true. There was no way in hell Anna would hand that out. She had to fight her over getting her to share her location with her. Right then the alarm bells were ringing, the same ones that she had the night he hit her.

Kyle sidled up a bit closer to her face, running a hand over her hair. "You know, Emily. It wasn't all bad, was it? Us, I mean?"

She shrugged. What was she meant to say to that?

"I mean, we had some good times, didn't we?"

"Kyle, my leg." She pointed. "I'm in a lot of pain. Do you think we could have this conversation in the truck?"

"You see because I was thinking that maybe, you know because of all of this, that maybe we could leave the courts behind. You know, work out our differences without them."

"It's a little late for that."

"No, I meant you and me. We don't have to go through with this divorce. We could uh... I could fix this. We could get away. You and me. You know, maybe go back to Hawaii, the same place we went on our honeymoon."

"Kyle, I just want to get in the truck."

"You wouldn't want that?"

She groaned in agony as another wave of pain rolled up her leg. "I didn't say I... Look, things between you and me just..."

"Don't say it."

"It's over, Kyle. Okay. I'm with Travis now."

"But it doesn't have to be that way. We can change. I can change," he said.

She sighed. "Kyle, just listen."

"NO!" he snapped. "You listen to me. You never listen to me."

Emily moved back ever so slightly, startled by his shift in demeanor.

"Kyle, please. Just help me to the truck."

"What, so you can go back and live with him? Force me to pay spousal support? Take away my kids? Make me look like a fool!" he said through gritted teeth.

She shook her head. "It's not like that."

"OF COURSE, IT IS!" he bellowed as she shifted back again, though now he moved with her, lifting his hand and tightening it into a ball. He shook it in her face. "You just want to take everything." He shook a finger. "Well, you're not going to. The kids. They're coming back with me."

"What are you talking about?"

He didn't respond to that but instead, let his actions do the talking as he quickly brought both hands up to her throat and slammed her head down on the asphalt. "Kyle! Stop it!" she managed to say before he began pressing on her larynx, trying to choke the life out of her.

Emily drove a fist into his ribs and clawed at his neck but he lifted his face away and continued to push down.

She was choking, trying to get air through her nose. Kyle put a stop to that by clamping a hand over her nose. Her eyes bulged, blood vessels burst in them as she struggled within his grip. His weight, his posture, and the way he was pushing down on her leg only made it harder to fight him off.

Her arms flailed, striking out desperately, only to see a swallowing darkness rushing in at the edge of her eyes. "Shhh! Shhhh!" Kyle kept hushing her as he loomed over, trying to choke, trying to rob, trying to kill her. "Just let go. Just let go," he snarled.

24

The situation was dire.

Bill could see how quickly it was all slipping through his grasp and spiraling out of control. And the worst part was, there wasn't a damn thing he could do about it. Not only was Plan B ruined with the death of Rooster and Bernard, but now the kid looked worse than ever. If she died before the rendezvous with Deputy Dipshit, he would never see that money.

Parked at the edge of a road, a few miles outside of Round Lake, New York, Bill had entered the RV to assess the situation. Pam and Marcus were like lost puppies unsure of what to do. He knew. He knew better than anyone else.

"You!" he said, charging toward Anna and sidestepping the vomit.

She was still on her knees gagging. He grabbed her by the wrist and lifted her, dragged her back into the bedroom, and went to throw her on the bed for the second time that day when he noticed something, a change of color, a shift on her watch.

"What the heck is this?"

A menu of icons was before him, menus he'd seen on smartphones, specifically on an iPhone. Anna tried to cover it with a hand but before she could do it, he ripped the Velcro sport strap off and took a few steps back. Holding it in his hand, he touched the green phone icon on the screen and the app opened with a dial pad. He looked at her, his lips pulling back.

"Who have you been speaking to?"

Anna said nothing but cowered back from him.

"Pam!" he bellowed. "Pam!" She was supposed to check her. Go through her pockets. Make sure she didn't have anything on her that could be used to track her. He hadn't thought about a smartwatch.

Pam entered the RV with a hand over her mouth, trying to avoid the smell.

"You had one job. One damn job. To check her. You see this!"

She squinted from the far end. She knew him well enough to not get close when he was this angry. "She's been talking to people."

"Through a watch?"

"No... through her ass. What do you think?"

"You know what, fuck you, Bill."

His nostrils flared. She'd tested him a few times. It had been a while since she had. He might have charged over there and reminded her of what happened when she spoke out of turn but right now, he wanted answers. His head snapped around.

"Who have you been speaking to?"

She shook her head. "I haven't."

"Don't lie to me!"

With all the commotion, Marcus came into the RV. He made his way down. "Let me look at it." Bill handed it to him while he scowled at the girl. He had a good mind to give her a beating.

"She's been messaging," he said, turning the watch around and showing him the iMessage feature. "Her mother, and by the looks of it someone called Travis."

"Travis Young," Bill said. "Kyle mentioned him. Said he might be a problem. He's a game warden from Bennington County."

"Yeah, well, according to these messages, he knows where she is and he's on his way."

"How?"

Bill wasn't too familiar with smartphones. He knew enough to place a call, and surf the net from his Android, but that was about it. He'd heard the fuss people made over Apple products but he thought it was just that, hype. Nothing more. "Well, there's a couple of ways. The Find My Device app, sharing Apple ID, or Share My Location."

"And you knew about this?"

"Everyone does."

"Oh my God, why me? Why do I get the fucking idiots!?"

"Screw you, Bill. You're the idiot. I just solved your damn problem."

"No, you didn't, you just told me we have one." He jabbed a finger at his chest. "I'm going to solve it. Now get out of the way!" Bill grabbed Anna by the wrist and she let out a squeal. He dragged her out of the bedroom through her vomit toward the door.

"Come on, Bill, she's just a kid."

"And you're just a moron."

Outside, he hauled Anna up over his shoulder in a fireman's lift and hustled over to his truck. He opened the door and threw her inside, then slammed the door and hit the key fob to lock it.

"What are you doing?" Marcus asked, following close behind.

"Going to get paid," he said, making his way around the truck to the driver's side.

"And what about us?" Marcus asked, standing by the equally confused Pam.

"You're going to deal with the problem," he said. "Set that watch down on the road, right over there. Get that RV out of the way and then get a rifle and enter the woods. When Warden Young gets out of his vehicle... shoot the bastard. Then join me in Round Lake at the boat launch. Don't come if you haven't killed him. Can you do that? Huh?"

"Sure but..."

"No buts. Just do it!"

"Can't I come with you, Bill?" Pam asked.

Hand on the door, he looked at her, snarling. "After your screw-up? You're lucky I haven't put a bullet in your head!" With that said, he hopped in and fired up the engine, and peeled out of there, scowling at the two of them.

Some days he wondered why he bothered.

25

The 21 Titan burst over a rise in the highway.

Its V8 engine roaring, a guttural noise piped out through the muffler. Travis gripped the wheel tight. Although he'd been white-knuckling it most of the way, he was now feeling even more hopeful as he made his approach on the green dot that had only updated a minute ago.

No change.

Good job, Anna.

She'd managed to delay them. Keep them in one spot.

Wanting to make sure he knew what situation he was heading into, he sent her a quick text. *Getting closer. Is everything still okay?*

No response came back.

It didn't mean there was a problem, as he was aware she was being watched and so she probably had to pick and choose her moments to respond, but it didn't make him feel any better.

As he came down Highway 9, a desolate stretch of road with thick forest on either side and no lighting except a full moon, Travis got this sinking feeling in his gut, the same one that came when he was called out to a 911 emergency that involved a domestic. It was the unexpected. The unknown. The situation could turn sour and any number of things could go wrong.

Travis glanced at his phone then back at the road.

He was almost upon the green dot.

Where was the RV?

There was no black truck.

What the hell? He slowed, easing off the gas, his senses on high alert.

Under the glow of the bright headlights, up ahead he could see the watch in the middle of the road.

Stopping twenty yards from it, he let the engine idle and scanned his field of vision. Getting out of the truck, he withdrew his Glock and placed both hands on it, keeping it low and ready. The wind howled. His eyes raked the wet terrain, going from the dense tree line to the watch.

"Damn it."

They'd found it and dumped it.

Even though he was certain that was the case, that they would have just tossed it and continued on their way, he couldn't be too careful. One round from a sniper lurking in the brush and it would be lights out.

Slowly moving forward, he kept checking his peripherals.

Travis tightened his grip on the gun, listening, every sense on high alert.

No sounds. No movements in the trees.

Stopping ten feet away, Travis began to back up instead of moving in on it. Call it a gut instinct, self-preservation, or a sixth sense that something wasn't right, he opted to get back in his truck.

The watch was no good to him now and...

Before the thought was processed.

Crack.

A round struck him in the left arm, sending him down and scrambling for cover.

Fresh adrenaline coursed through his system.

Another round echoed, and another. Travis dashed for the rear of his vehicle. Although it was too dark to see anyone, he had seen a muzzle flash off to his left and fired several defensive rounds in that direction.

Pain streaked through his body.

He took up a position behind the truck and quickly checked the injury. He reached over and felt his shoulder. Based on the level of pain, he figured it had just clipped him, taking a chunk of flesh but nothing fatal. Another round echoed, this time off to his right, followed by one more off to his left.

He ignored the pain and forced himself to think.

There were two assailants and he was pinned down in the middle of the road. It wouldn't take them long to work their way up. He had to act fast. Make a decision. There was no easy way through it and there was a good possibility he'd be killed but he had to decide. Stay or risk dashing into the forest?

Neither was a good option.

More rounds hit the truck as they tried to force him out of hiding.

Travis adjusted his grip on the Glock and eyed the road, focusing on the thick brush. Getting into a runner's pose, as if he was at the starting gate of a race, he exhaled hard several times and then burst out, firing wildly before diving into the brush and rolling down an embankment and landing hard against a tree.

Around him, gunshots erupted.

Through the darkness, he saw a muzzle flash from roughly fifty yards.

Adrenaline surging, Travis scrambled across the forest floor. He got into a crouch and made his way around, zigzagging his way through the forest, trying to stay as small and quiet as possible. As his uniform was a forest green, he blended in with ease.

"Marcus?" a female yelled. "Did you get him?"

Finally, a name.

"Get the RV started, Pam," Marcus replied, announcing his location. Travis homed in on it and sprinted towards the sound of his voice, his legs brushing up against the underbrush, gun by his side, at the ready.

Multiple rounds tore into the trees, sending bark in every direction.

Travis pressed his back against a tree, waiting for the chorus of gunfire to stop. The second it went quiet, he peered out and through the trees saw a woman emerge on the road and make a run for it. He was too far away to take her out, and between them was Marcus. There were no words exchanged between the two. They both had the same agenda. And only one of them was walking out of these woods alive. Travis darted out of his hiding spot, firing several times, and took cover again behind another thick tree. Marcus returned fire.

Travis could see his dark shape sneaking nearer, moving from tree to tree.

In the distance, he heard an engine roar to life.

Was Anna in that? He wouldn't fail her now. When he

heard Marcus load another magazine into his gun, he got a bead on him. Instead of rush at him and risk being shot, he slipped down to the forest floor, using the thick underbrush as cover. Wiggling forward on his elbows and knees, he shifted into a new position, closer, at least two trees nearer to Marcus who was looking beyond, at the tree he'd gone behind.

Closing one eye, he brought up the gun and peered through the sight.

This shot had to count.

Drawing a deep breath, he slowly let it out as he squeezed the trigger.

Crack. Crack. Marcus crumpled, groaning loudly.

Travis waited a few seconds to be sure he wasn't a danger before getting up and making his way over. Cautiously, he approached to find him on his back, gripping his stomach. "Where is she?" Travis asked.

He looked as if he wanted to say something but couldn't form words.

"Where is she!" he bellowed.

An engine revved and the sound of tires moving caught his attention.

Travis fired one more shot into Marcus to put him out of his misery before sprinting out of the forest back onto the road. Up ahead, no more than twenty yards, he saw the front of the RV pulling out of a small opening in the forest.

Pam looked his way and gunned it.

Travis was closer to the RV than his truck. He slipped his gun back into his holster and burst into a sprint as the RV emerged and tried to pull away. The downside to such a heavy vehicle was speed. It was like a heavy bus that was fine once it got up to speed but was slower out of the gate.

That worked to his advantage.

Chest heaving, his thighs burned as he chased after it, focusing on the ladder on the back which led up to the roof. The cloudy toxic fumes of the diesel engine wafted in his face as he stretched out his arms and grasped a rung of the ladder.

The RV increased its speed.

His boots dragged behind as he held on for dear life.

Using every ounce of upper body strength, he reached for the next rung of the ladder and managed to pull his feet up onto a ridge on the back of the vehicle. There was no window on the back. Clinging to the ladder, he looked back at his truck and took a second to catch his breath. The RV bounced as it rumbled south.

Secure, he began to climb until he could see the roof.

A gust blew in his face.

Besides a few air vents, the top was smooth and at the speed she was going, he was liable to slide off. Figuring Anna was inside, and having no idea of when the RV might stop, or if it would, he climbed up. Staying as low as he could, Travis moved forward as the wind rushed over him, threatening to send him off at any second. Had she been making lots of turns, or aware that he was on top, he might not have been able to claw his way forward.

Once he made it near the front, Travis peered over the edge and noticed a vertical steel bar that was part of the RV's awning. It was within arm's reach of the door. Reaching down, he took hold of it and swung his legs over, and slipped down just enough that he could reach for the handle. Grunting from the effort, and trying to stay on, he latched on to the steel. Pulling it wide, he heard Pam curse.

Before he could get in, she swerved erratically trying to

shake him loose. Blood rushed in his ears, fear pulsated. He could feel his grip getting weaker.

Clinging to the vertical pole, Travis was whipped from side to side, his shoulder slamming into the RV. He knew he couldn't hold on much longer.

With each swerve he was slipping further down.

It was now or never.

As the door swung open for a third time with the swerve of the RV, Travis reached inside for the handle he could see through a thin vertical window. That gave him enough support to swing his body inside onto one of the three steps that led into the cabin.

"You motherfu—" Pam screamed, unable to take her hands off the wheel. She could only try to stop him from entering by swerving and making him almost fall out.

His pulse jumped.

There was a handle on either side of the short staircase allowing people a way to support themselves as they entered. Using both, he thrust himself forward against her.

His body slammed into her. The RV took a hard swerve to the left as he pushed her face against the window.

"Stop the RV!"

"Screw you!"

She yanked the wheel, sending him tumbling back. Travis managed to hold on to the passenger seat and pull himself up. As he was doing that, Pam reached across for a small revolver that she'd set on the dashboard.

Leaning back, Travis kicked her arm. She shrieked.

As he tried to get his gun out of his holster, Pam kept moving the RV from side to side in such a sharp, erratic manner that he had to hold on or he'd tumble out.

Doing the next best thing, Travis latched on to her. He

slipped his arm around her neck, trying to place her in a chokehold. "Stop the vehicle!" he bellowed as the RV swerved all over the road. As she accelerated, even more, he reached down, unbuckled her belt, and yanked her out of the seat, throwing her down, out of the RV. He heard her body hit the asphalt with a sickening thud.

Sliding into the seat, Travis crushed the brake just as the RV was about to veer off the road into the tree line.

The brakes squealed and everything inside the RV shot forward: plates, cutlery, ashtrays, anything that wasn't locked down came tumbling forward, a loud and chaotic clatter. Travis lurched forward over the large wheel, breathing hard.

He got out of the seat and looked back.

"Anna?!"

No answer.

He made his way to the bedroom and cleared the bathroom.

Nothing. No one. She wasn't there.

He climbed down the steps and out of the RV and looked back.

Maybe thirty yards back on the road, Pam was laying facing down. She was still alive, barely. He saw her move as he approached, pulling his weapon. "Where is she?" he asked as he got closer. She was a bloody mess, the skin on the side of her face and palms looked as if it had been sanded off. Her shirt was torn, and one of her shoes was off. Her left arm was twisted in an ungodly way, broken, a bloody bone protruding.

"Fuck you," she spat.

Crouching beside her, he took the gun and placed it against the side of her head.

"Is she worth losing your life?"

Pam turned her face toward him, snarling, a mash-up of

grit, dirt, and blood. "Mine is already over. Go ahead. Shoot me." He fired off a round behind him, simply to get her attention.

"The next one goes in you. Tell me where she is!"

A pause.

"TELL ME!"

She began laughing, blood drooling from her lower lip.

"You'll never see that kid again."

"Is she dead?"

"She's sick. Really bad."

The diabetes travel pack. It was in the Titan. Damn it.

"Where is she? I won't ask again."

"And I'm not telling you."

He had a good mind to put a round in her head but that wouldn't help Anna.

"Fine." Losing his temper, he stood up and looked at her, then placed his boot on her broken arm and pressed down hard, causing her to scream in agony. He found no pleasure in her pain but without a location, Anna was as good as dead.

"Ahhrghhhh!"

"That's not the answer."

The longer she waited to tell him, the more he bore down on her.

"Round Lake. She's at Round Lake. Get off!"

He released his foot.

"Where in Round Lake?"

"At the boat launch. Bill's taking her there to do an exchange with Kyle."

Without wasting another minute, he turned and went back to the RV.

"Hey. HEY! Don't leave me here. Come back!"

Travis remained silent.

He slipped into the seat and did a U-turn in the road to head back to the truck. He'd need the diabetic pack. By the time he had it facing north, Pam had staggered to her feet, grasping a small revolver in an ankle holster. Blood gushing from her arm and her face looking like a truck had hit it, she withdrew the gun and pointed it at him, firing once, twice, three times. The rounds speared the window and he swerved.

Instead of crashing into the ditch, he hit the gas and drove at her, full tilt, slamming into her, not slowing for even a second as he felt the thud of her body go under. The RV bounced ever so slightly as it crushed her beneath the wheels.

He glanced in his mirror.

Now, she was nothing more than roadkill.

No longer able to harm another girl. No longer a threat.

26

Emily desperately fumbled with his duty belt.

Working off instincts, years of being married to him, and having him come on to her at the end of the day in full uniform — she'd become all too familiar with what was on the belt, the multiple pockets, and where everything was stored: magazines, pepper spray, Glock, baton, Taser, and a Spyderco knife. Whether it was the continual jostling and her firing a fist into his ribs, but he didn't notice as her finger unclipped the button that held in the knife, the only thing that she was able to reach. As she was clawing at it, terrified of losing consciousness, her fingernail caught one of the screws on the stainless-steel folding knife and managed to extract it just enough that she could grab it.

Thumbing the edge, she forced the blade out of its steel sleeve, and as the light in her eyes was beginning to fade from the pressure of his thumbs, Emily jammed the blade into Kyles's thigh.

His mouth widened in a wide O and a scream erupted. Instantly, his hands withdrew and his back arched in a spasm of agony. Knowing that wasn't going to be enough, she pulled it out and jammed it in again, but this time twisting it.

What came next was the hardest blow to the face she'd ever felt.

Far harder than the one he gave her the day before she left him.

Like a mallet hitting its mark, his fist collided with her jaw. He unleashed another furious right hook. At least she saw that one coming. If she hadn't moved just when she did, there was no doubt in her mind he would have knocked her clean out. Fortunately, his fist slipped off her orbital bone, sending a spike of pain through her skull. He followed through with one more left that broke her nose, then a right, and another that split her lip, before rolling off and staggering to his feet.

He stumbled, falling back against a truck and gripping the knife in his thigh.

The world blurred, a hazy kaleidoscope of sound and color.

Her skull throbbed hard; every part of her body screamed.

Emily spat blood out like a fountain, most of it landing on her face.

Broken, battered, she rolled onto her side, dribbled more blood, and glanced at him crying in agony as he tried to summon the courage to pull the knife out.

He looked at her with more hatred than she'd ever seen. "You bitch!"

Kyle looked worse than any rabid animal. He had this menacing stare that made her know what he would do once he got his hands on her again.

With one swift pull, he extracted the knife, letting out

another loud wail before dropping down from the pain. She heard the knife clatter against the ground. Knowing he'd left the truck door open, she moved onto her knees and crawled forward, away.

Pain coursed through her worse than anything she'd ever felt.

She tried to yell for help but there was no one to hear her as the words came out more of a whisper than a cry.

Using the support of a bumper, Emily managed to wobble to her feet and stagger around the cars over to the truck. All the while she kept looking back expecting to see Kyle approaching. He was still on the ground, trying to tie off his leg with the sleeve he'd ripped off his shirt.

Moving as fast as she could, she stumbled forward, each time setting her bad leg down and screaming in agony. Where were the others? Where was anyone? The highway was nothing more now than a graveyard of steel bones.

Coming up behind the rear of the truck, Emily could hear footsteps.

She shuffled. Terror quickened her pulse as she got close to the open door.

More footsteps, this time coming up the rear even faster.

Casting a glance over her shoulder she just caught sight of him as Kyle slammed into her, bouncing her body off the door like a pinball.

Emily hit the ground hard, knocking the wind out of her.

The world spun, and darkness set in.

Unconscious for an unknown amount of time, she awoke to the sensation of moving as her body was dragged along the asphalt.

"You just couldn't let it go, could you?"

Her eyes opened and shut. Each time, she saw him dragging her. *Move Emily, move!*

But she couldn't.

She was exhausted.

Her body ached and screamed in agony with every tug.

A bright light shone in her eyes as she looked back.

That's when she knew where he was taking her, out in front of his truck, under the glow of the lights, to a place where he could inflict more punishment and look into her eyes as she took her final breath.

Kyle released her and stumbled away, talking to himself.

A vehicle rushed by on the hard shoulder, another followed, but neither stopped. Had they seen her? Were they even paying attention? Did they think she was just another victim of the event?

She cried out in anguish but her voice was lost in the wind.

Emily twisted, looking towards the truck as he reached in and pulled out a shotgun. He slammed the door shut and racked it. "You just don't learn. But I'm going to show you." He was staggering toward her, leg bleeding. She watched him approach.

Like an inmate waiting for a warden to flip the switch on the electric chair, she knew this was it. It was over.

She'd failed.

Now whether it was the vehicles that sped past earlier that made him not look, or maybe he was so fixated on killing her, he didn't care. But the sound of an engine grew louder. Behind him, a truck came barreling toward him, not letting up for even a second.

Emily's eyes widened.

He was oblivious, muttering something under his breath.

All spit and fury as he angled the shotgun toward her, preparing to...

The truck struck him, sending him soaring through the air, and landing hard.

Brakes squealed.

Rubber burned then Carla hopped out, hurrying toward her.

"Emily!"

"Carla," she groaned through the panicked haze of her mind.

Her sister looked at her face, her leg and throat, and tears welled in her eyes. "That bastard." She looked off toward where Kyle lay. "Come on, let's get you out of here," she said, sliding her arms underneath Emily's and helping her up. The pain was enough to make her pass out. How she hadn't already was astonishing. The body was capable of taking only so much punishment. With trembling hands, Emily held on to her sister as she winced in pain. With her standing on a wobbly leg and dragging the other, they twisted around heading back to the truck.

They hadn't made it a few steps when...

"Emily!"

Her head turned at the sound of his gruff voice. It wasn't fear this time, it was anger. Struggling to rise, Kyle pulled up his knees then collapsed. "Don't look at him," Carla said, moving her a few feet more.

"EMILY!"

His persistent voice triggered something in her, a deep hatred, a realization that it would never be over even if they drove away, unless...

Her gaze fell upon the shotgun. She waved off her sister. "Let go."

"Emily. He's done."

"No. Not yet."

"He's done. It's over."

She pushed her away and stumbled toward the shotgun, shuffling forward with renewed sense of purpose. She dropped down to one knee and picked it up. Carla looked on, aware of what she was about to do. All Emily could think about was his hands around her throat, the look in his eyes, Anna, and what he had tried to do.

"You won't steal my spirit, you won't take the kids, you won't ever touch me again," she muttered under her breath as she summoned the courage to face her fear.

Wobbling on one leg, she moved towards him, her bad leg dragging behind.

Kyle was on his hands and knees, blood oozing out of his mouth, internal bleeding that no doubt would rob him of life even if they did drive away. He'd already racked the shotgun so all she needed to do was aim and shoot.

Angling it down, she shouted his name. "KYLE!"

She wanted to look into his eyes. She wanted him to see her courage.

It was about taking back her life.

Taking back power.

A final act of victory over her abuser.

Kyle glanced at her and chuckled.

Was he shocked? "You don't have the..."

Boom.

The round struck his shoulder, sending him back.

His body slumped sideways. Groans came from him as he stared up into the sky.

"Never. Never again, will you touch me."

Boom. She fired once more. The round obliterated his thigh.

"Nor will you ever harm our kids."

She loomed over him, aimed at his face, and delivered the final blow.

27

"C'mon! Pick up," Bill said, clutching his phone tightly. Why wasn't he answering? He'd phoned Kyle three times to find out where he was. Although they hadn't agreed on a time to meet, he figured he would let him know that he was waiting. The sooner this was over, the better. Once he had the money, he would head south to the Caribbean, somewhere warm, somewhere he could disappear.

Forget Pam, forget Marcus. They were nothing but dead weights.

Without an official release, he was going to need every cent of the five hundred thousand to start a new life. He couldn't afford mistakes and mistakes were what those two morons were experts at.

Standing in the bow of a 28-foot Boston Whaler fishing boat that was thirty feet from the dock, he stared at the huge lake covered in dead fish. It smelled worse than any city fish market.

A rancid and vile odor made breathing difficult.

Near his feet, the kid was curled into a ball, shaking and sweating. She'd been complaining about a fast heartbeat, dizziness, and shortness of breath. If she died before he arrived, he would dump her body in the lake and make up some story for Kyle that Marcus had her, and wanted him to meet at some other location to pick her up. There was a chance he might buy it, probably not though.

For now, he was waiting on either Kyle or Pam and Marcus to show. Several vehicles had been by, none of which were them. He didn't need to wonder if Kyle would get law enforcement involved, as he had as much to lose as him. And even if he did, even if he pulled a fast one, where could he muster up a group to help? The boys in blue were too busy dealing with this mess.

From what he'd seen on his way down, the event had escalated further. Bill had seen large numbers of sheep, horses, and cattle lying dead in fields. That only boosted his reasons to get away from the mainland.

Whatever this was, it was spreading and fast.

A set of headlights shone in the distance as a truck veered into the parking lot at the boat launch. He'd found several boats moored, abandoned. He'd manually started the double engines on the back of one, then took it out a short distance from the shore so he could negotiate yet at the same time make a quick exit across the lake if need be.

Squinting in the darkness, he couldn't tell if it was Kyle or not. Though he was sure he caught a glimpse of a police emblem on the side of the truck. "Hey kid, kid, wake up!" he said, shaking her. "Looks like your pops is here. A few minutes from now, you'll be as right as rain. No harm. No foul." She looked at him but didn't move. Her eyes closed again.

He shrugged. Once she was back with Kyle, she was his problem.

He fired up the engines and the boat glided through the water, getting a little closer, mostly so he could see who it was. If it was local PD, he would turn and gun it out of there. With no lights in the lot, he was at the mercy of whoever was coming down the dock. Killing the engine so he could hear, he shouted, "Kyle? That you?"

There was no answer.

He turned on one of the boat spotlights and shone it at the dock.

The light swept over the figure approaching.

The stranger lifted an arm. His uniform gave him away. That wasn't Kyle. It was the game warden. He gritted his teeth, fuming.

I should have known those twerps couldn't do one simple task.

"Bring Anna back to the shore, Bill."

"Can't do that. The kid is my paycheck. I'll let her go once I collect."

"You know Kyle is never going to give you that money."

"He will if he wants his daughter alive."

"No, I mean he won't because he isn't coming. He's dead."

The words hung there, driving deep into his core like a sharp knife.

There was a long pause. Was this a lie? Bill tried Kyle's phone number. Again, it went to voicemail. He would have answered by now.

"All I want is her. I don't care about you. Drop her off and you can leave."

"And let state pursue me later? I think not. No. I get my money..." he grabbed the girl and pulled her up and pressed a revolver against her head. "Or she dies."

Travis was quick to reply. "If I don't get this insulin in her, she's going to die." He lifted a package and Bill glared at it. "Then what will you have as leverage?"

That bastard.

He had him at a stalemate.

The only way he was getting that money was if she was alive. And one look at her and she was already sitting at death's door. "So, give me the insulin and I'll inject it."

"It doesn't work that way, Bill. If I hand it to you, I won't see her again. You know it. So, you have to decide what you want more. Money or freedom?"

Both had been offered at the start by Kyle.

After losing Rooster and Bernard, all he had left was the promise of money, and now he was meant to give that up...? It was clear he wasn't getting that money. No one could come up with that kind of cash under these circumstances. "Fuck!" he said under his breath, realizing he was screwed. The only thing left was his freedom. There was no way in hell he was giving that up.

Bill's eyes roamed the boats and his mind started making connections. If he brought her in, the warden would pursue him but if he... Bill stared at the rancid water covered by birds and fish. He looked at Anna. Maybe he was a good-for-nothing criminal, a lost soul gone astray, and maybe he'd made a series of wrong choices that he would one day be held accountable for, but not today, today was his, today — he held in his hands her life. And if he couldn't be okay, then maybe she could.

"You want her?" he bellowed.

The warden nodded.

"Then come get her!" he shouted, taking the kid with both hands and throwing her over into the water. Just as he expected, the warden unbuckled his duty belt, threw off his hat, removed his shoes, and dove into the water. That would buy him more than enough time to escape.

Bill fired up the engines. The propellers churned up frothy water as he navigated away, holding to the one thing he valued more than money, his freedom.

And deep down, that was all he ever really wanted.

28

The frigid April water shocked him to the bone as Travis swam through the gunk of death. He'd seen Anna struggling to stay above the water. When he was within twenty feet of her, she disappeared beneath. He dove down searching, scanning the putrid waters before breaking the surface for air.

His head whipped around, searching again before he went back under, this time focusing on a mass of black sinking before him. Seeing her face, Travis latched on to an arm and dragged her upward.

Bursting out, he gasped, drawing in lungfuls of air.

"Anna." She was out cold. Wrapping an arm around her, he swam back. In the distance, he could see Bill escaping. He wanted nothing more than to get his hands on him but between saving her or capturing him, Anna mattered more. He was nothing but a two-bit criminal, Kyle's puppet who would disappear into the shadows, going underground like the maggot he was. Never to return. And if did, he'd find himself locked up for the rest of his life. Even he knew that.

Soaked to the bone, Travis dragged Anna out of the muck onto the dock and assessed her to see whether he needed to give full CPR or just rescue breathing. He placed his hand on her forehead and began tapping on her collarbone. "Anna. Anna. Can you hear me?"

He pulled back her head and did a carotid pulse check. She still had a pulse but it was weak and she wasn't breathing normally.

He brought his mouth down to hers and gave one breath every three seconds for two minutes. He assessed again, checking for a pulse. If there hadn't been a pulse and she wasn't breathing, he would have immediately begun CPR but there was an improvement. "Come on. That's it."

Anna coughed hard, sending a fountain of water out.

"That's it, kiddo. All right. I got yah."

He turned her onto her side, allowing more water to seep out the corner of her mouth. While she was coming to, he reached for the insulin pack and unzipped it. Inside were alcohol wipes, several vials of insulin, and orange-capped syringes with 28-gauge needles. Emily had already walked him through the process of giving her an injection just in case there were any issues while she was away.

"Anna. Hey, I've got your insulin here," he said as he pulled out what she needed. He held up the insulin to the light of the moon to make sure it was clear. Good. It wasn't cloudy. As it was rapid-acting insulin it would take anywhere from ten to fifteen minutes to kick in after injection to lower her blood sugar. It had to be injected into the fat just beneath the skin, usually the stomach, thighs, or buttocks.

Travis lifted her top, exposing her stomach. He popped the caps off the top and bottom of the syringe, tore open an alcohol wipe, and wiped the top of the vial. Hurrying, he poked the needle into the vial through the rubber stopper. Once he'd done that, he pushed the plunger to inject air into the bottle, then turned the bottle upside down and withdrew the right number of units. Travis held it up and tapped it to make sure bubbles in the syringe went to the top. He pushed the syringe to release the bubbles back into the bottle before pulling back to the right amount. Emily had drilled it into him how important it was to get it right.

Before he injected, he dabbed her skin with another wipe to make sure it was clean.

Travis brought the syringe over, pinched two or three inches of skin, and then inserted it and injected the insulin.

"There you go, sweetheart. You're gonna be okay."

EPILOGUE

As the sun rose over the state of Vermont in the early hours of the next morning, Travis arrived in Eden Falls with Anna, tired but very much alive. He'd already phoned Steph and made arrangements to bring Lucas to Emily's home. News of Emily's survival and Kyle's demise had reached him moments before his confrontation on the dock in Round Lake. He never asked how Kyle died, or who killed him, only how Emily was doing. Whatever happened, in his mind, Kyle had it coming to him.

Karma was a bitch and she knew how to repay those who wronged her.

As he veered around the bend on Meadowbrook Drive that led up to the cul-de-sac, he noticed how quiet the road was. The panic he'd witnessed in various towns throughout the night had subsided as many retreated to the safety of family.

Family.

That was what it was all about.

Not much else mattered in the face of a disaster.

They had only scraped the surface over twenty-four hours but as daylight took charge and news broke, Eden Falls and its residents were about to find out how bad life would become.

Travis smiled as Anna slept on the passenger side of the Titan, a vehicle he would have to get repaired before its return. Beyond time recouping in Round Lake, and a few pit stops along the way for gas and a washroom, they'd pretty much driven back without stopping. As he pulled up outside, his warden truck was a familiar and welcome sight. Carla had told him she would bring it back and true to her word she had.

Easing off the gas, he stopped the vehicle and stuck the gear in park before shaking Anna. "Hey, time to wake up, sleepyhead. We're home."

"Ugh?" she said, pawing at her eyes and peering out.

"Now your mom is in poor shape, okay, so don't be panicked when you see her. She'll heal up." He got out and opened the passenger side and helped her down. As he was doing that, the door opened and Steph stepped outside, closing the door behind her. She had a bathrobe on and was holding it together with one hand near her neck. "Hey sis," he said, making his way up. "How is she?"

"Sleeping. He beat her up pretty bad." She looked past him and glanced down. "Anna." Steph dropped to a crouch and gave her a big hug and then led them inside. "I'll put the kettle on," she said.

Anna kicked off her shoes and went straight into the living room and plunked herself down on the couch, curling up into a ball. Travis stood in the space between the hallway and the living room. He leaned up against the door frame, feeling a wave of exhaustion. He'd been firing on all cylinders since this had started and now his body was ready to rest.

"You look tired. You should sleep," Steph said.

"Yeah. Maybe later. You making coffee?"

Steph smiled as she went back into the kitchen and he followed her.

"How's Lucas?" She'd told him what he'd done. It was brave but killing a man at his age, something like that was liable to stay with him for years.

"Surprisingly well." Steph leaned back against the kitchen counter, her brow furrowing as she got this distant look in her eyes. "I wouldn't be here if it wasn't for what he did."

"And you?" Travis asked.

She shrugged, turning away and putting a heap of instant coffee into a cup. "I don't think I've fully processed it."

"There's plenty of time. If you need someone to talk to..."

"I'll be sure not to go to you," she said, then chuckled.

"I thought I heard talking."

Travis smiled at the sight of Carla entering the kitchen. Barefoot, she was wearing grey jogging bottoms with the word VERMONT down the leg, and a white T-shirt. He rose and hugged her. "Good to see you made it back in one piece."

"You know, Carla..."

"Don't, Travis. It's okay. We learn and move on."

He nodded. He still felt a sense of guilt over the way things had played out. She made her way past him and collected a cup out of the cupboard to make her drink.

"Carla. Did you bring Danny back?"

"Of course," she said without looking at him. Although she said things were okay, he could tell from the way she looked at him that it wasn't true. But that was to be expected. It would take time to rebuild trust.

"Where are we going to bury him?" Steph asked, tears welling in her eyes.

"We'll get to that later today. Leave that to me."

"Travis." He turned to see Emily at the bottom of the stairs, leaning against the banister. Her face was swollen, black and blue, and her lips cut. Kyle had really given her a beating. He felt anger rise inside, wishing he could have been there to stop him.

"Hey, I told you not to get out of bed," Carla said, brushing past Travis before he reached her. "Come on now, you need to go back upstairs."

"I want to see her," Emily said.

"Like this?" Carla asked.

"Let her be," Travis said, making his way over and hugging Emily. She winced at the slightest touch. They stood there for a moment, embracing and just taking a second to let it sink in that they were both safe. Emily pulled away, gave a strained smile, and hobbled into the living room using a crutch under one arm. There was a cast on her leg where she'd already received medical attention. She set the crutch down and sat down beside Anna and ran a hand over her hair. "Hey baby," she said in a soft voice.

Anna's tired eyes opened and then widened. "Mom."

The three of them watched as they embraced and cried hard.

Giving them alone time, Travis went back into the kitchen to collect his coffee. He took a stool at the kitchen island and yawned, hands running over his eyes. He picked up the remote to the small flatscreen and turned it on, keeping the volume low. There wasn't one channel that wasn't tuned into the event.

As he sipped at his drink that morning, the reality of their new world started to crystalize. Video from all around the world streamed farms where all the livestock was dead. If that wasn't bad enough, news broadcast stations showed thousands of dead pets. None had survived.

Slowly, the sound of a reporter talking drew in the others. They quickly surrounded him, each curious and speechless at what this meant for them, for the country, for the world.

"The animals, they're all dead?"

No one knew what to say or what this would mean.

They were facing an unknown world, a terrifying future that brought only questions. What now? No one could tell what lay ahead or how bad it would get, only that the battle to survive wasn't over, it had only just begun.

THANK YOU FOR READING

Extinct: The Great Dying Book One

Primal: Book 2 is out now

Please take a second to leave a review, it's really appreciated.

Thanks kindly, Jack.

A PLEA

Thank you for reading Extinct: The Great Dying Book 1. If you enjoyed the book, I would really appreciate it if you would consider leaving a review. Without reviews, an author's books are virtually invisible on the retail sites. It also lets me know what you liked. It also motivates me to write more books. You can leave a review by visiting the book's page. I would greatly appreciate it. It only takes a couple of seconds.

Thank you — **Jack Hunt**

READERS TEAM

Thank you for buying Extinct: The Great Dying Book 1, published by Direct Response Publishing.

Go to the link below to receive special offers, bonus content, and news about new Jack Hunt's books. Sign up for the newsletter. http://www.jackhuntbooks.com/signup

ABOUT THE AUTHOR

Jack Hunt is the International Bestselling Author of over sixty novels. Jack lives on the East coast of North America. If you haven't joined ***Jack Hunt's Private Facebook Group*** just do a search on facebook to find it. This gives readers a way to chat with Jack, see cover reveals, enter contests and receive give-aways, and stay updated on upcoming releases. There is also his main facebook page below if you want to browse. facebook.com/jackhuntauthor

www.jackhuntbooks.com
jhuntauthor@gmail.com

Printed in Great Britain
by Amazon